FOODWORKS

FOOD

*Over 100 Science
Activities and
Fascinating Facts That
Explore the Magic of Food*

WORKS

from the
Ontario Science Centre

Illustrated by
Linda Hendry

Addison-Wesley Publishing Company, Inc.

*Reading, Massachusetts • Menlo Park, California • New York
Don Mills, Ontario • Wokingham, England • Amsterdam • Bonn
Sidney • Singapore • Tokyo • Madrid • San Juan • Paris
Seoul • Milan • Mexico City • Taipei*

The Ontario Science Centre in Toronto, Canada, is a vast science arcade. Its three connected buildings are filled with more than 500 exhibits. You can play with them, test yourself against them, try experiments with them. The aim is to let you explore, experience, and enjoy science.

Although a visit to the Science Centre is unique, science itself is all around us. And you don't need a laboratory full of equipment to discover it. Now you can have the Ontario Science Centre spirit at home with *Foodworks*. All you need for the activities in this book are a little curiosity and items found in most every home kitchen. These activities have been enthusiastically tried by thousands of readers. We hope you have fun doing them, too.

Other books in the Ontario Science Centre series available from Addison-Wesley Publishing Company:
SCIENCEWORKS

Series Editor: Carol Gold
Writers: Mary Donev
　　　　 Stef Donev
　　　　 Carol Gold

All Ontario Science Centre projects are the product of the entire staff, whose help in producing this book is gratefully acknowledged.

Library of Congress Cataloging-in-Publication Data

Foodworks : over 100 science activities and fascinating
　　facts that explore the magic of food.

　　Includes index.
　　Summary: Discusses the role of food, what it does and
how it acts inside the body, through explanatory text and
science activities.
　　1. Food—Juvenile literature.　2. Nutrition—Juvenile
literature.　3. Science—Experiments—Juvenile literature.
[1. Food.　2. Food—Experiments.　3. Nutrition.
4. Experiments]　I. Hendry, Linda, ill.　II. Ontario
Science Centre.
TX355.F66　1987　　　641.3　　　87-1796
ISBN 0-201-11470-4

First published in Canada in 1986 by Kids Can Press,
Toronto, Ontario.
First published in the U.S. in 1987 by Addison-Wesley
Publishing Company, Inc., Reading, Massachusetts.

Book design by Michael Solomon
Cover artwork by Linda Hendry

　　8　9　10　11　12　13-AL-95949392
Eighth printing, August 1992

CONTENTS

"TRY THIS" ACTIVITIES

FOODWORKS

FOOD FOR A YEAR

COULD you eat all the food in these shopping carts?

Sure. It'll take you just about a year.

There's about 1 tonne (ton) of food in these carts. That's the amount of food the average North American (including males and females, adults and children) eats in one year.

That's about 1.25 million calories of energy or 3400 a day. The average person needs 2400 calories a day to stay alive and healthy. Does that mean some people are eating more food than they need?

Here's what's in those shopping carts:

- 67 kg (147 pounds) of bread, rolls, oatmeal, rice, etc.
- 105 kg (231 pounds) of beef, pork, poultry, fish, eggs, dried beans and nuts
- 100 kg (220 pounds) of milk products, including 12 L (3 gallons) of ice cream
- 287 kg (632 pounds) of fruit and vegetables, including 70 kg (154 pounds) of potatoes
- 311 kg (685 pounds) of other stuff, including 71 kg (156 pounds) of pop and 40 kg (88 pounds) of sugar

FOOD FOOD FOOD

ALTHOUGH 500 million tonnes (tons) of crops are harvested each year, a great deal of it doesn't make it to your plate—or anyone else's. Where does the rest of the food go?

Animals eat most of it. Between 75 and 95 per cent of the grains grown in North America goes into barns for animals to eat.

A lot of food is lost to disease or to pests like insects and rodents. A single rat, for example, eats 11 kg (24.2 pounds) of grain in a year.

We even lose food as it's processed. Fibre is lost when grain is refined. Vitamins are lost when food is canned, frozen or cooked. Waste from vegetables could be put to better use—fed to animals instead of being thrown out.

Even when the food does make it all the way to your dinner table, some of it is still lost. North Americans are known for buying and serving too much food. Where does it go? Into the garbage. There are about 10 garbage cans full of wasted food for each person in North America a year. That's about 250 kg (550 pounds) of garbage—a quarter of what you started with in all those shopping baskets.

SWALLOW THIS

URE, you've travelled before—to school or maybe to the other side of the world. But have you ever travelled down a human throat?

Imagine you're a hamburger. Just what happens after you and your buns get bitten?

First, you get chewed. Spit, or saliva, has a special chemical called an enzyme which starts digesting food as it's chewed.

Getting down a throat, or esophagus, is not a simple matter. As you start off, a small flap of tissue called the epiglottis closes over the entrance to the windpipe. Let's face it. You may be a great-tasting hamburger, but no body wants you in its lungs.

Next, you get some heavy duty bear hugs from muscles in the esophagus. They don't believe you can find your way to the stomach unless they push you there. These waves of pushing are called peristalsis.

Finally, you get a little elbow room. You slide into the stomach and it shuts behind you. You can't get out of this 1 L (1 quart) pouch. You're churned around like clothes in a washing machine. The stomach muscles also think squeezing is just what a hamburger needs. You meet up with more enzymes and a liquid called hydrochloric acid. These break you down into even smaller bits.

After a couple of hours, you look like a real mess—more soup than hamburger. Then the stomach opens up an exit and you're glad to be on your way.

Not so fast. The trip isn't over yet. You're being squeezed into the small intestine—and it's not that small. It must be 6 or 7 m (20 or 22 feet) long in here! More chemicals are dumped on you to help digestion along, first enzymes from the pancreas and then bile from the liver.

Finally the body decides you're ready to be used. Protein, glucose, fats and water are pulled out of you by lots of folds in the small intestine that look like fingers sticking out. These "villi" are just waiting to sop up all your nutrients and pass them along to the bloodstream.

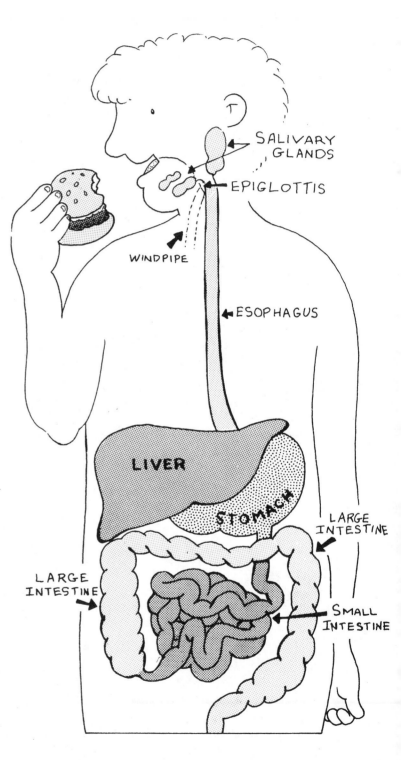

The small intestine has a motto: "If you can't use it, eliminate it." But it's the large intestine that handles the waste disposal job. It's wider than the small intestine and only about 1 m (3 feet) long. It's got a heavy duty job to do. It finishes soaking up water and minerals. Then it collects what's left of you—the waste products that the body can't use—and pushes them out, along with a lot of dead bacteria, in the form of feces or stool.

What an exciting journey for a hamburger to take—and you didn't even need a ticket.

Digestion in space
Even though digestion is helped by gravity, there's no problem eating in space where there is no gravity. Muscle movement, or peristalsis, still gets food where it needs to go.

TRY THIS

Spit on it
To see how the digestion process works, try this experiment. Take a small piece of meat and put it in a tiny container. Put enough of your saliva in with it to cover the meat. Let it stand for a day. What do you see?

A window to the stomach
A French Canadian, Alexis St. Martin, was accidentally shot in his side on June 6, 1822. Dr. Beaumont treated him, and although St. Martin recovered, he had an opening nearly 2 cm (¾ inch) across that led directly into his stomach. Dr. Beaumont used him as human guinea pig to study how the stomach actually works. St. Martin lived with the hole in his stomach until he died in 1880, at the age of 82.

Dr. William Beaumont examining the hole in Alexis St. Martin's stomach.

THINGS THAT GO GROWL IN THE STOMACH

A BURP is just a bit of wind
Forced upward from the chest.
But when it takes a downward path,
It's then called flatulence.

But what makes that wind?
You may well ask,
'Tis a question most perplexing.

It's the foods you eat
And stuff you drink
Being mushed up in digesting.

And as it's dissolved
By stomach walls
You can hear the food a-churning.

But at other times
Your stomach growls:
"It's food for which I'm a-yearning."

Your burps and flatulence (or farts) are caused by trapped air and gas. Stomach growls, called borborygmus, are made by your intestines contracting. The louder the sounds, the harder they're working.

Everyone is different, especially when it comes to burps, flatulence and growls. A meal that will turn a friend's stomach into a rock and roll band might leave yours as quiet as a turned-off radio.

TRY THIS
Stomach turn-ons
Find out what turns a stomach on. Put your ear against a friend's stomach before a meal. What do you hear? Record your observations in detail and then listen again after trying some of the foods below. Is there any difference in sound? Does your friend have more flatulence after some foods than others?

onions	peanuts	melons
raw apples	cooked cabbage	chocolate
baked beans	radishes	lettuce
milk	cucumbers	eggs
cauliflower		

Bigger and better burps
Burps are just your body's way of getting rid of excess gas. Can you make bigger burps by increasing the amount of gas in your stomach? Try chewing gum, gulping down air or a carbonated beverage.

Pick a cure—any cure

Have you ever had the hiccoughs so long you thought you'd never talk again without sounding like a broken record? One man, Charles Osborne, started hiccoughing in 1922 and is still going. Although he says he's had a normal life, including being married and having eight children, he can't keep his false teeth in.

What causes hiccoughs? Lots of things, ranging from getting upset to eating a meal that's too spicy. Whatever the cause, the result is the same. Your diaphragm, a large muscle across your chest which moves up and down when you breathe, starts contracting in jerks. To stop your hiccoughs, all you have to do is shock your diaphragm out of its contractions.

There are lots of cures for hiccoughs, and every single one of them works—sometimes. Next time you start hiccoughing try one of these diaphragm shockers:

- a good fright
- eating a spoonful of crushed ice
- pressing in just a little bit on your closed eyeballs
- swallowing a large spoonful of dried breadcrumbs
- gulping a tablespoon of peanut butter
- eating a spoonful of sugar
- sucking on a lemon
- drinking a large glass of water in one gulp
- holding your breath
- standing on your head and breathing through your nose.

THE CASE OF THE MISSING TEETH

YOUR teeth are well suited to the kind of food you eat. So are animals' teeth. Meat-eaters have ripping teeth, plant eaters have flattened grinding teeth and so on.

An animal's teeth and jaws can tell a lot about their owner, even if the rest of the animal isn't there. By examining them, scientists can often figure out what the animal ate—even an extinct animal like the dinosaur—and what kind of animal the teeth belonged to.

How good are your tooth detective skills. See if you can match up these sets of teeth with their toothless owners. Answers on page 91.

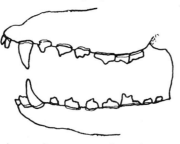

1. I'm a carnivore (meat eater) and my teeth help me kill my prey. They have to be able to tear the meat and crunch bones. They'd better have sharp ridges and pointed, triangular edges. I don't have to chew my meat well, so my molars (back teeth) aren't important for that. Instead, they work like scissors to cut off pieces of meat and are useful for crushing bones.

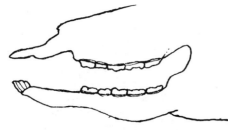

2. One way to tell that I'm a herbivore (plant eater) is that my teeth never stop growing. Plants are tough and need to be ground up so I need flat teeth with hard ridges, like millstones.

3. Who needs strong teeth when you eat insects? I'm an insectivore, and the bugs I eat are small and really easy to digest.

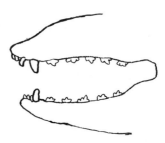

4. Find any teeth that are small with barbs pointing towards the back of the mouth? They'll do just fine for a fish eater like me. I swallow the slippery creatures whole and just need my teeth to hang onto them until I can get them down.

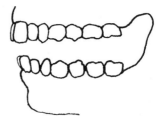

5. I'm an omnivore—I eat everything, so my teeth don't need to be quite as specialized. My molars (back teeth) are fairly low, with rounded edges so I can crush and chew a lot of different foods. Some of us omnivores have longer canine teeth (the ones in the front corners of our jaws) for biting or self-defense. You'll see those in monkeys. Others have canines that are good for rooting, as in pigs.

OPEN WIDE

FIND a mirror and open wide. Your mouthful of pearly whites are precision tools you probably take for granted. Each kind of tooth is well suited to the job it has to do.

Your incisors and cuspids have single roots and single cutting edges for biting and tearing through foods.

Your bicuspids and molars have two or more roots. They have broad, chewing, grinding surfaces for chewing and crushing food to aid digestion.

Did you know?

- Prehistoric children didn't eat refined sugars so they had almost no tooth decay.
- According to *The Guinness Book of World Records*, the strongest teeth in the world belong to a Belgian man named John "Hercules" Passis. In 1977 he raised a 233 kg (513 pound) weight 15 cm (6 inches) off the ground with his teeth. Two years later, he kept a helicopter from taking off using a mouth harness.
- Your teeth wear down more as you get older and the amount they wear down depends on your diet. Primitive people's teeth showed more wear because they ate rough food. Today, your food is softer, so your teeth wear down less.
- People don't chew up and down. They chew side to side, something like cows do.
- The people with the largest teeth are the Inuit and Australian Aborigines. The smallest teeth belong to African Bushmen and Laplanders.
- According to *The Guinness Book of World Records*, the most valuable tooth belonged to Sir Isaac Newton. It was bought for $1300 in 1816 by a nobleman who wore it in a ring.

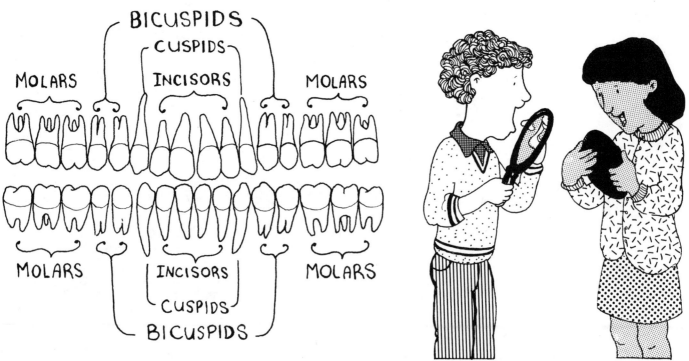

Some snacks that are bad for your teeth	
cake, cookies, donuts	figs
candy	raisins
ice cream	grapes
apple juice	gum
cocoa	marshmallows
soft drinks, sweetened juices	peanut butter
dates	jam or jelly

Some snacks that are good for your teeth	
nuts	corn chips
popcorn (plain)	cheese
carrots	oranges
celery	tomatoes
potato chips	milk
	olives

TRY THIS

Bite with your chewers
See if you can make your teeth do a different job than they were made for. Bite into an apple with your molars and chew it with your incisors and cuspids.

The acid test
Plaque is bacteria on your teeth. It feeds on sugar and gives off an acid as waste. The acid is what makes holes or cavities in your teeth. To see how easily acid can eat through teeth, place pieces of eggshell in two cups. Like teeth, eggshell is mostly made of calcium. Cover the eggshell in one cup with a bit of water and cover the other with vinegar, which is an acid. Leave the eggshells until all the water and vinegar evaporate. What condition are they in? Is there anything left in the cup?

Green teeth?
Your dentist has probably stained your teeth red to show where you missed brushing. You can do the same thing at home by brushing and then swishing food colouring around in your mouth (but don't swallow it!). The colour sticks best to plaque, so it's darker where you missed brushing. If you want to look really frightening, the splotchy unbrushed look is great—especially for Hallowe'en! (Your tongue may turn colour too, but it washes off fairly easily.)

DEAR **Dr. Food:** *Why do I sometimes feel hungry?*
When your stomach is empty, it starts to contract. It starts with a rhythm of about three contractions per minute but soon they happen more often, last longer and are stronger. This sends a message to your brain: "Send food down here. Fast!"

Dear Dr. Food: *If I didn't have a stomach would I still get hungry?*
Strangely enough, yes, you would! People who have had their stomachs surgically removed still feel hungry at times. Why? Your stomach works together with a part of your brain called the appestat to tell you you've got that empty feeling. Even without your stomach's help, the appestat still works. Part of the appestat tells you: "Start eating, you're hungry." When you've had enough to eat, another part of the appestat says, "Stop now, you're full."

No one is really sure how the appestat works. It might be like the thermostat in your house, which tells your furnace to turn on the heat because the house is getting cold and then shuts the furnace off when it's warm enough. Your appestat might turn your hunger on—telling your body it needs to burn fuel to keep you going—when the temperature of your blood goes down slightly. When the temperature goes up, it shuts off.

Your appestat might also work as a sensor. When there's not enough glucose (a form of sugar) in your blood, it shouts, "CHOW TIME!"

Dear Doctor Food: *Sometimes after I've eaten, I feel like the food is sitting in my stomach like a rock.*
The way you eat and digest food is often affected by the way you feel. Were you upset or angry when you got that rock-in-the-stomach feeling?

Scientists discovered that how we feel affects our digestion by observing a man named Tom. Tom couldn't swallow food because his esophagus, the

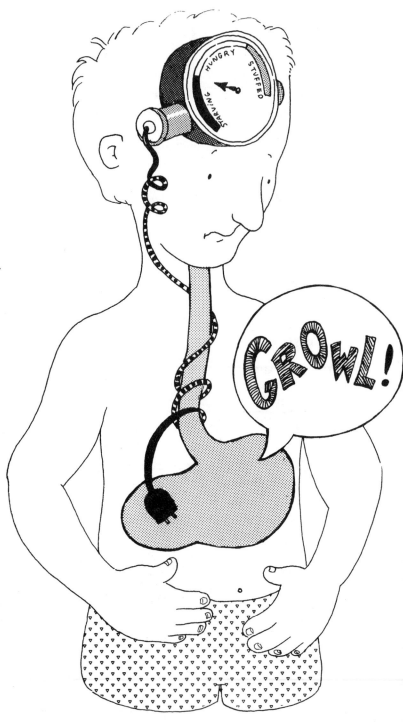

tube through which food passes on its way to the stomach, was damaged. He learned how to chew his food and then take it out of his mouth and put it in a special rubber tube that went directly into his stomach.

Tom lived like this for years, and one day he agreed to be part of a study. Two doctors looked through the tube into his stomach and watched what happened every time Tom ate.

When Tom got mad, the doctors noticed that his stomach lining changed from pink to bright red and his stomach juices flowed more quickly. If he then ate a meal, the food passed through his stomach even faster than it usually would.

When Tom was unhappy, afraid or depressed, his stomach also changed colours, but instead of bright red, it turned very pale. There were also fewer stomach juices. Even when Tom ate, the normal amount of digestive juices weren't there and his food just sat there for hours, undigested.

So the next time you sit down to eat—whether it's peanut butter or stewed liver in spinach sauce—remember that how you feel may affect your meal as much as how you feel about the meal itself.

TRY THIS

Appetite tester
What turns your appetite on? Think of a lemon. Does it make you feel hungry? Now think of chocolate cake. How do you feel? Do you notice any changes in your stomach or your mouth? Do you react differently when you do this experiment right after a big meal?

ANIMAL GOURMETS

How about a cup of blood for dinner? Or maybe some rotten meat? They may sound disgusting to you, but for some animals, they're real treats!

Bloodsucker!
Beware of vampire bats! While their victims sleep, the bats suck their blood!

True? Not entirely.

While vampire bats in South America do like a nice snack of warm blood from sleeping prey, they don't suck the blood out. Instead, the 10 cm (4 inch) mammal uses its teeth to make a razor sharp cut in the unsuspecting victim while it sleeps. Although only about the size of a mouse, it laps up its own weight—about 28 g (1 ounce)—in blood in one night with its long tongue.

Young bats are less experienced in this kind of cafeteria style dining and are often so awkward they wake up their dinner! As the bat gets older, its technique gets smoother and it can feast all night. It keeps the blood flowing with a special anti-coagulant in its saliva.

Some bats seem to be part pig. They overeat so much that they're too heavy to fly.

Frog food
When is a frog not just a little green amphibian who likes to sit on a lily pad catching flies? When it's an ornate horned frog. This green and red frog from Argentina not only has a head that looks like it's half mouth, but it has an appetite to match. This cannibal will devour anything it can grab and pull into its mouth with its sticky tongue—including other frogs!

Look out, Kermit!

Not fussy
A turkey vulture never met a meal it didn't like, especially with a topping of maggots and flies.

Hardly a picky eater, the vulture is a regular garbage disposal unit. It feasts on dead and rotting animal carcasses. Pass the ketchup!

Paramedic maggots
Maggots are hardly picky eaters either. Before the 20th century, people often put maggots (the larva or worm-like stage a fly goes through before reaching adulthood) on their wounds. The maggots ate the dead and infected tissue, which made the wound cleaner and allowed it to heal faster. This lessened the risk of infection.

Of course, it didn't do much for your popularity.

Garbage collectors of the sea
Albatross scoop dead fish and animals and other garbage out of the oceans and eat it. They can also drink sea water and survive because of a special gland in their noses that gets ride of excess salt. One adventurous albatross from the South Pacific, with a wingspan of more than 3 m (10 feet), will fly as far as 4000 km (2500 miles) in search of food for its young. It's called—what else—the wandering albatross.

Move over, Mr. T
Do not adjust your television set. You have just entered the cockroach zone.

A type of cockroach informally called the "TV roach" (its Latin name is *Supella supellectilium*) lives in the back of TV sets and eats insulation, glue and other parts. It's so happy with its life there, it never leaves the set looking for other food. Or maybe it just likes the reruns.

ARE you omnivorous? If you are, you'll eat everything but the kitchen sink. A few animals, like people, are **omnivores**. They eat both meat and plants.

Most animals specialize in one or the other. A lion wouldn't think of having vegetable soup and a salad for dinner. Being a **carnivore**, it likes meat and plenty of it.

An elephant, on the other hand, turns its trunk up at a delicacy like a steak or a hot dog. It's a **herbivore**, so give it a bowl of grass, hold the Thousand Island dressing, please.

The amount an animal eats depends on more than just its size. Because plants have less nutritional value than meat, a herbivore has to eat more, and more often, than a carnivore does.

A lion living in the zoo will eat 1/35 of its own body weight each day. For a 160 kg (350 pound) lion, that's about 5 kg (11 pounds) of meat a day, adding up to 1825 kg (4025 pounds) a year.

In one year, a 5500 kg (12,125 pound) pachyderm packs in:

1600 loaves of bread

50 000 kg (110,225 pounds) of hay

3000 cabbages, apples, carrots and other vegetables

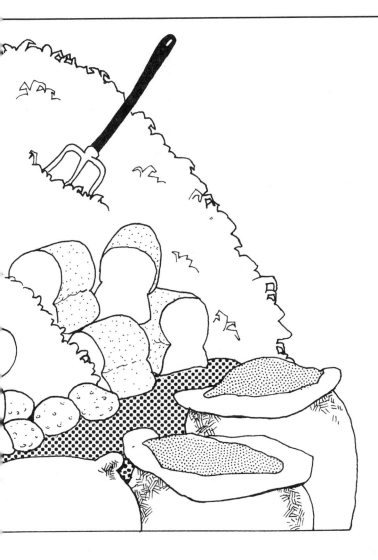

5500 kg (12,125 pounds) of alfalfa
2000 potatoes
6800 L (193 bushels) of grain
70 000 L (15,400 gallons) of water

That works out to about 1/20 of its own body weight or 275 kg (600 pounds) a day per elephant. It's no wonder they can sit wherever they want!

The smaller the animal, the more it eats in relation to its size. A field mouse, for example, eats as much as it weighs everyday. Imagine how big a refrigerator you'd need if you ate YOUR weight in food each day!

TRY THIS

Big eater?

How much do you eat each day in relation to your weight? Weigh yourself and weigh your meals. Don't forget the snacks. Divide your weight by the amount of food you eat to find out.

FOOD RERUNS

AVE you ever enjoyed a meal so much, you wish you could eat it again?

Some animals run instant replays of their favourite meals. After swallowing, they regurgitate the partly digested food, chew it and then swallow it again as a second course.

Cows are one kind of animal that recycles its food. They're called ruminants. They have stomachs with four separate compartments.

When the cow takes a bite of food, she sends it down to the first compartment (called the rumen) without even chewing it. Bacteria that live there get to work on the grass and break down the cellulose in it. Then, whenever she feels like chewing, the cow brings some of the semi-digested food—now called cud— back up to her mouth and chomps on it for a while.

The next time she swallows the food, it goes to another stomach compartment and stays down, pass-ing through the remaining compartments and getting a little more digested in each one.

Not all animals that rerun dinner are ruminants, however. The great horned owl, for example, re-gurgitates round pellets about seven hours after it eats. These pellets contain undigested bones and fur from the animals the owl has eaten. What happens to these pellets? The owl eats them again to get any leftover food value from them.

Rabbits recycle from the other end. They eat their own droppings—but only the green ones. These pellets have undigested cellulose in them. The only way for the rabbit to get the nutrients out of the cellulose is to eat the green droppings. The second time they pass through the rabbit's system, they're digested.

Talk about leftovers!

Rumen

TRY THIS

Recycle it

You can be a food recycler too! Recycling means to use something again. Why not make leftover food into nutrient rich soil for your plants? It's easy with this kitchen compost pile.

You'll need:
a waterproof container, such as an old milk carton
waterproof tape
scissors
a knife or food blender
food leftovers
potting soil or dirt from the garden

1. Use the tape to seal the open ends of the milk carton.
2. Lay the milk carton on its side.
3. Cut a flap in the upper side large enough to allow you to reach inside with a spoon.
4. Gather up food scraps that are left over from a meal.
5. Cut them up or, with permission, put them through a blender so they are shorter than 3 cm (1 inch) and are quite thin. Drain any garbage that seems too sloppy or wet.
6. Spread your recycled food over the bottom of the container. Cover it with a thin layer of soil.
7. Each day, stir the mixture well and then add another layer of food and soil until you've filled the container to about 3 cm (1 inch) from the top.
8. Set the filled carton aside and let the bacteria in the mixture continue to break the food down. You can help things along by stirring your mix every day. If it seems like it's drying up, add a little bit of water, but nothing else.

In about three weeks you'll have crumbly, brown soil that's full of nutrients. You can sprinkle it around plants in your house or garden as a special, nutritious treat you made yourself. If you add it to a vegetable garden, you'll wind up eating the nutrients again yourself!

 EXT time someone accuses you of having weird eating habits, tell them about these animals ...

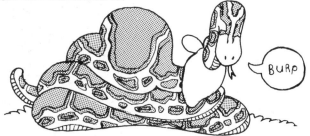

Big eater

Your mother may have told you never to eat anything bigger than your head—but that's only if you're not a Burmese python. It swallows meals four times the size of its head in one gulp.

The python isn't a dainty eater. This 7 m (23 foot) long snake can grab a small deer or a wild pig in its mouth, quickly wrap its body around its meal and squeeze until the animal suffocates. One big mouthful and dinner vanishes.

Once the python has eaten, it won't eat again until it's digested what's in its stomach. For one stuffed snake, that took two years!

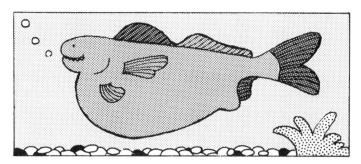

Stuffed fish

The blackswallower, a deep-sea fish, also swallows prey larger than itself. To make room for a big meal, it moves its heart and gills off to the side. Moveable teeth in its throat push the food down to a stomach that stretches enough to hold fish twice its size.

Dangerous weapons

Two animals who should be in the army are vultures and archerfish.

Some vultures like ostrich eggs, but find the thick shells impossible to break open with their beaks. So they drop rocks on the eggs to smash the shells.

The archerfish likes to play "shoot the fly" for dinner. It spits water at insects sitting on branches above the pond and then grabs them when they hit the surface. That's more difficult than it sounds. Why? Try the experiment next page to find out.

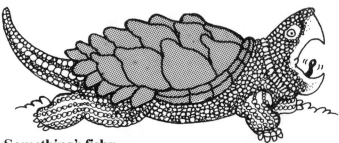

Something's fishy

The alligator snapping turtle didn't get its name because it *looks* like an alligator, but because it *eats* them!

Besides alligators and ducks, it also enjoys a fresh fish dinner, which it catches with its own built-in fishing lure. The turtle has an appendage that looks just like a red worm on its lower jaw. When it opens its huge mouth, it wiggles this "worm." The moving worm attracts passing fish who try to catch it for dinner. Once they swim near the turtle's mouth, it's not long before they're the catch of the day.

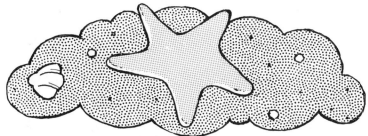

Stomach turner

Some people really get into eating—and so do some animals. The starfish throws itself into a meal. When it finds a tasty morsel, such as a clam, the starfish pushes its stomach out through its mouth, turns it inside out and throws it on top of the clam. The stomach immediately starts digesting the clam, without even waiting until it's back inside.

What an eyeful

Are eyes only for seeing? Toads and frogs use their eyes to help them eat! When a toad or frog swallows, it closes its eyelids and presses its eyeballs onto the roof of its mouth. This squeezes its tongue, forcing the food down and into its stomach.

Spaghetti anyone?

Birds eat half their weight in food each day. Young birds have even bigger appetites. A young robin eats as much as 5m (16 feet) of worms a day.

TRY THIS

The archerfish test

It's hard enough to swat a bug when both of you are out of the water. But an archerfish is *in* the water shooting at a bug *outside*, which makes things even more difficult. That's because light bends when it travels from air into water, so the archerfish has a distorted view of the bug's position. How good is your aim when looking through water? Try this test to find out.

You'll need:
a large jar filled with water
a piece of paper
a pencil

1. Put the jar of water on a table.
2. Draw an X on the sheet of paper and lay it on the table behind the jar.
3. Look through the jar of water and try to touch the centre of the X with the tip of the pencil.

31

YOU ARE THE FOOD

YOU don't feel it, you don't even notice it, but you're being eaten, little by little, right now! And you can't even see most of the creatures that are munching on you.

No matter how much soap you use, you always have bacteria on you and in you. In fact, you have more microbes—microscopic organisms such as bacteria, yeast and viruses—on and in your body than there are people on the entire Earth! You have them on your skin and hair, inside your nose, mouth and in your intestines. And you provide their breakfast, lunch and dinner.

To give you an idea of their size, it would take 9 trillion medium-sized bacteria to fill a box the size of a package of chewing gum sticks. There are about 300 000 of these tiny microbes on any dime-sized section of your skin.

Fortunately, most of the bacteria in your body are not only necessary, they're friendly. The microbes on your skin, for instance, are scavengers. They look for other bacteria to eat and feed on your dead skin cells.

The bacteria in your intestines, called Escherichia coli, or E. coli for short, eat some of the leftover fibre that your body can't digest. As they eat, they break the fibre down and make its nutrients available to you. At the same time, they produce vitamin K and vitamin B12. Vitamin K helps your blood clot when you cut yourself, and vitamin B12 protects you from anemia, a sickness that makes you very run down and tired.

Although keeping yourself clean is important, scientists have discovered there's such a thing as getting rid of too many germs. They've raised super clean animals; animals that are totally microbe free. Rather than being healthier, these animals get sick more easily! Without the microbes that should be in their bodies, the animals have trouble fighting off the germs that don't belong. Microbe-free animals also have weaker hearts and their intestines don't work the way they should.

So not only do you have to feed your body to stay healthy, you have to feed your body's bacteria. Some things you eat, like yogurt and cheese, contain bacteria that are good for you because they build up the bacteria in your body.

You're eaten not only by things you can't see but by things you *can* see—like mosquitos and black flies. Although you look at them as pests, they look at your blood as a meal. Without you and other animals to snack on, their lives just wouldn't be liveable.

So next time someone asks, "What's eating you?"—tell them.

TRY THIS

What you can't do

There is no simple, safe way for you to see the microbes that live on you. You could see them individually with a powerful light microscope or an electron microscope or in numbers by growing them in a sterile nutrient solution, but those methods require specialized equipment. However there is a way for you to see another kind of microscopic organism.

What you can do: grow mould

You'll need:

a clean pie plate
a piece of paper towel
a piece of bread (white bread is easiest to observe but takes longer)
plastic wrap

1. Wet the paper towel and lay it on the pie plate.
2. Place the slice of bread on it.
3. Cover it all with plastic wrap and put in in a dark place.
4. Leave it for a few days, then look at it. Try looking at it through a magnifying glass or with a microscope, if you have one. You're seeing clusters of tiny microscopic organisms called moulds. Moulds are a different kind of organism from the ones that live on you; they're more plant than animal. But like your body microbes, moulds are so small that you can't see them, even though they're in the air and on surfaces all around you. When they find a suitable environment such as some nice damp bread, they grow in great numbers and become visible.

GETTING THE BUGS OUT

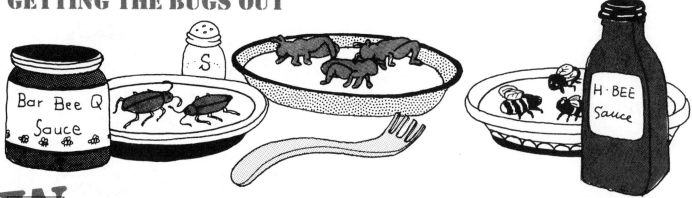

WHAT's for dinner tonight? How about cockroach casserole, beetle burgers or termite fried chicken.

Sound scrumptious? If not, you don't know what you're missing. There are people for whom the thought of termite fried chicken sets tastebuds to watering and lips to smacking. For others, the cockroach is a gourmet treat. Ditto the termite.

Insects are a popular source of food the world over. Termites, ants, butterflies, stinkbugs, grasshoppers, cicadas, bees and just about every other insect you can name is eaten and enjoyed somewhere. And why not? By most standards, insects measure up to any other food. They are nutritious, a good source of protein and minerals. They're delicious too. Termites taste just like pineapple, and some people swear that chicken fried in termite oil is just as good as chicken fried in butter. Baked bees, which are dry and flaky like breakfast cereal, have a pleasant, nutty flavour. Cockroaches, lightly salted, perform a delightful tap dance on the tongue.

But, isn't it true that insects are ridden with disease, you protest? Yes, a few insects—body lice, assasin bugs, biting flies, mosquitoes and fleas—do carry viruses, parasites and bacteria. But these bugs only transmit disease by biting, or when their excretions or bodily fluids are rubbed into the skin. Proper cooking renders most disease-carrying bugs harmless.

Many people also think that insects are filthy. Actually, insects are no dirtier than any other animal people eat. Pigs love dirt, but who, for this reason, refuses to eat bacon and ham? When properly washed, insect meat is just as clean as beef or pork or chicken. The cockroach, for example, may look dirty and greasy, but in fact it is one of the cleanest of all insects.

Still not tempted by insects? Surprise—you eat them all the time without knowing it. Supermarket lettuce, no matter how well washed, is home to plant lice (aphids). In many cases, those tiny brown and black specks that you see in flour and bread are fragments of granary weevils, flour beetles and Mediterranean flour moths. Citrus fruits are frequently dotted with small brown spots that are actually insects. The "tongues" of these insects stick into the peel of the fruit, so that even when you scrape off the insects, their "tongues" remain inside the pulp. Insects are the hidden spice in our food.

Not only do we eat insects, we eat—and enjoy—what they produce. Honey, of course, is a product of the bee—and a very intimate one at that. Bees swallow nectar from flowers and carry it back in the stomach to the hive where they "vomit" it into the honeycomb. So why do we eat bee "vomit" and ignore the bees?

Insects could well be the food of the future. Because they grow quickly, produce high-quality meat and are inexpensive to raise, insects would make an ideal food for space travel. The best livestock animal for space farming could be the drugstore beetle. This hardy bug is not a fussy eater and will consume everything from flour to coffee beans to the poison strychnine. Unfortunately, the drugstore beetle can also chew through sheet lead, so an orbiting beetle farm would have to be well-sealed to prevent the bugs from escaping and dining out on the spacecraft's wiring and walls.

TRY THIS

If you don't like bugs, how about worms?

Why not try earth worms for lunch for a change? They have more protein than T-bone steak and no bone or gristle. To get them ready for eating, put them (live) into fresh peat moss for 24 hours. This gives them a chance to clean out their insides. Then boil your clean wiggly worms in water and lemon. Next, bake them on a tray for 10 minutes in a 175° C (350° F) oven. They make a crunchy snack. Or maybe you'd like to try a sk-worm sandwich?

Be adventurous!

Take a tour of ethnic grocery stores and the gourmet section of your neighbourhood supermarket and try some unusual delicacies. If you can talk your parents into buying chocolate-covered grasshoppers or candied wasp eggs, make sure you buy a small package. You wouldn't want good food to go to waste.

A MATTER OF TASTE

WHAT'S your favourite breakfast? Do you like a bowl of cornflakes and milk with some juice? Or maybe some pancakes with maple syrup and bacon on the side?

If you lived in India or China or France, you wouldn't eat such things for breakfast. In fact, you might never have even heard of cornflakes or pancakes!

Kids in Israel wake up to a meal of cottage cheese, yogurt, hardboiled eggs, olives, tomatoes, cucumbers, bread or pita (circles of flat bread that open into a pocket) and fruit—usually oranges. Sometimes they have sardines or smoked fish.

If you lived in India, you'd start your day with a lentil pancake called a *dosa*. It's stuffed with a *massala*, a mixture of potatoes, onion and spices. Or you might try *idli* (steamed rice pancakes). Instead of syrup, you'd use either coconut-based or spicy dipping sauces.

Feel like hot cereal? In India, it's spicy hot too. *Uppama* is something like porridge cooked with onions and curry spices. You might top your breakfast off with sweet lime juice.

The Chinese like *congee* for breakfast. It's a thick rice gruel which is often topped with barbequed pork and green onions.

In France, small breakfasts are the rule. Croissants or baguettes (long bread sticks) are washed down with *café au lait*. The English, on the other hand, like a really big breakfast, starting with cold cereal. Then, bring on the fried eggs, bacon and sausages, fried tomatoes, fried mushrooms, toast and marmalade!

Ever tried soup for breakfast? The Japanese love clear soup flavoured with a soybean paste called *miso*. Another favourite breakfast soup, called *miso-shiru* is made of tofu, seaweed, scallions or radishes. Of course, rice sprinkled with *nori* (dried seaweed) is great to eat on the side.

TRY THIS

Make your own congee

How about a Chinese breakfast? You can make congee for the family one morning . . . but you'll have to get up early to cook it.

You'll need:
250 mL (1 c) rice (not instant)
2 L (8 c) water
large saucepan with lid
cooked bits of chicken, fish, meat or vegetables
(optional)

1. Put the rice and water in the saucepan and partly cover the pan.
2. Bring the water to a boil on high heat, then turn the heat down to low and put the lid completely on the pan.
3. Cook for 40 minutes or longer until the rice has absorbed all the water and becomes very soft.
4. Serve plain or with little bits of fish, chicken, meat or vegetables on top.

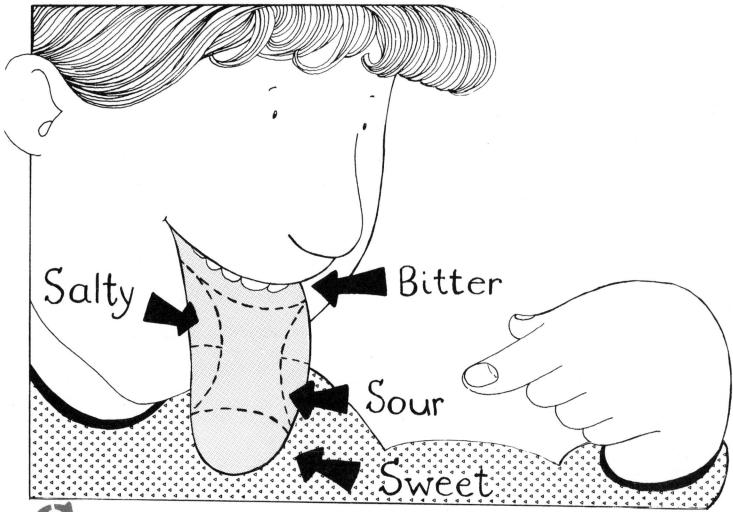

 STICK your tongue out and look at it. Can you count the bumps on it? They're full of taste buds, about 9000 of them.

Taste buds helped warn primitive people whether the leaf or berry or bush they were eating was safe. If it tasted bad, it probably was bad, possibly poisonous, so they spit it out. Babies still do the same thing: they taste everything.

Today, you count on your taste buds to determine how good something is, not how safe it is. Your taste buds help you tell the difference between chocolate and vanilla, cheese and chicken—even Pepsi and Coke. And they do it all with just four tastes: bitter, sour, sweet and salt.

The smell, feel, texture and look of food also contributes to how good—or bad—it tastes. That's why food tastes so bland and boring when you have a cold. You can't smell it.

If you've ever had the bad luck to munch on a hot chili pepper, you'll know that you don't taste anything. Instead it feels as if your tongue is on fire. Spicy foods like curry or hot peppers create "heat" in your mouth by reacting with nerve endings on your tongue.

snacks are easiest to identify, even with your nose plugged?

Try the experiment again with a few changes. Keep the blindfold on, but don't hold your nose. Instead, rub a little vanilla extract or peanut butter or cinnamon on your upper lip. Do you think it will change the scores?

TRY THIS

The tasty tongue

Place a little sugar on different parts of your tongue. When do you actually taste it? Do the same with lemon juice, salt, tonic water. Try other tastes too.

Try this experiment again after you've sucked on an ice cube for a minute or so. Does it make any difference?

The nose knows

Prepare a sample plate of bite-sized snacks, every-thing from carrots and radishes to bologna and chocolate. Then, with friends, take turns tasting them while you wear a blindfold and hold your nose so you can neither see nor smell what you are eating. Try and figure out what you are actually tasting. Keep score to see which of you has the best sense of taste. Which

Eye see how good it is

Ask your parents if you can fix an experimental rain-bow meal. Use a little food colouring to create blue milk, green gravy, red mashed potatoes, etc. You can even put celery in a glass of water with food colouring in it to change it as well. Who in the family eats it? Did they feel it changed the taste of the food to have it presented in living colour?

DON'T LET THE FOOD FEARS GET YOU

HAVE you ever been terrified by a tomato? Petrified by a potato? Grossed out by garlic? If you have, then you've been a victim of FOOD FEARS! But you're not alone. Millions of people have been victims of FOOD FEARS over the years, fears of some of the nicest foods you could eat.

Take, for example, the tomato. When it was introduced to Europe by Spanish explorers who brought it back from Central America in the 1500s, it became quite popular—but only for a while. Then it became unpopular. Even worse, people thought it was poisonous. They believed that if you ate a tomato you'd be dead before midnight.

Why? No one knows for sure. It may have been because the tomato is a member of the nightshade family, which includes many poisonous plants. In fact, tomato leaves are toxic and should not be eaten.

At the height of the tomato's unpopularity, people still grew tomato plants, but only as decoration. Then on September 26, 1820, in Salem, Oregon, Colonel Robert G. Johnson finally defeated the tomato food fear. As hundreds of people watched, he stood on the courthouse steps and ate an entire basket of tomatoes. He didn't die. He didn't even get sick.

When people found out that tomatoes weren't poisonous they went to the other extreme. They decided tomatoes were a medicine. In the 1830s, Dr. Miles's Compound Extract of Tomato was sold throughout most of the United States. It was guaranteed to cure anything that ailed you. Today, we still use Dr. Miles's Compound as a flavouring ... but now we call it ketchup.

Another FOOD FEAR victim is the potato. Mashed, hashed, baked, boiled or french fried, the potato is one of the world's favourite foods. But back in the 1500s, when potatoes were first brought to Europe from Peru by returning Spanish explorers,

many people couldn't stand them. They were convinced that potatoes were poisonous. In fact, in 1610 in the Burgundy region of France, a law was passed making eating potatoes illegal because the medical experts and scientists of the day believed that if you ate too many potatoes you'd catch leprosy. While that wasn't true, potatoes, like tomatoes, are members of the nightshade family. If growing potatoes are exposed to light, they can develop green spots, which are concentrations of nightshade toxin and can make you sick if you eat them.

While the French didn't know beans about potatoes, they knew about garlic. Like the Greeks and many other cultures, the French loved garlic and the special flavour it gives so many foods. They also realized that it is a very healthy food.

The British, however, hated it. They thought it was worse than poisonous: they considered it low class. One of the worst names a Briton could call someone back then was: "Garlic eater!"

Chocolate was another victim of FOOD FEARS. In many Central American mountain villages in the 1700s, chocolate was considered to be the devil's drink. If you drank it, the devil would be able to control you.

Corn wasn't considered devilish or poisonous—just inedible. Even today in parts of Europe, corn is considered food for cattle, not people.

Some foods weren't feared, just misunderstood. When tea was first introduced into North America in the 1700s, many people boiled the leaves in water, threw out the water and served the tea leaves with sugar or syrup.

THREE FOOD MYSTERIES

HY do people in hot climates eat spicy hot food?

To cool off—honest!

Mexican and South American cooking calls for a lot of hot chili peppers or sauces. East Indian recipes call for hot curries. Why would people in hot climates want to eat hot foods?

Back before people had refrigerators, freezers or even TV dinners, food spoiled quickly, especially in hot climates. The hot spices helped make the food last longer. And even when the food did start to go bad, the flavour of the spices hid the bad tastes.

But that's not all. Really spicy food makes you sweat, and when the sweat evaporates, it cools you off.

If you lived in the North Pole, would you want to sweat after every meal?

Who invented noodles?

When you hear words like spaghetti, lasagna or fettucini, you probably think of Italy. After all, that's the land where noodles were invented, right?

Wrong!

Noodles were invented by the Chinese. But the Italians fell in love with the idea of turning grain into pasta (noodles) and then covering the pasta with different sauces. The Italian version became popular across Europe and North America.

But while the Italians only made pasta from wheat, the Chinese also made noodles out of rice. That meant they could have twice as many varieties as the Italians.

Why aren't Chinese noodles as well-known as the Italian ones? During the hundreds of years since Italy adopted noodles, many travellers have visited and eaten there and many Italians have settled in other countries, taking their recipes with them. China, on the other hand, was comparatively isolated from the rest of the world for a long time. Chinese food has only "travelled" to the rest of the world in the last hundred years or so.

Why don't the Chinese eat cheese?
Chinese delicacies include snakes, locust, eels, almost everything—except cheese. The Chinese don't drink much milk, either.

If you live in North America or Europe, that probably comes as a surprise. In these parts of the world, most people, including many adults, drink milk and everyone knows how good it is for you.

In the rest of the world, however, most people older than about three years have trouble digesting milk. Why? Milk is a complete food for baby mammals, the group humans belong to. But after a calf, puppy, whale, etc. grows too old to nurse from its mother, there's no place for it to get milk to drink. So its body stops producing the enzymes needed to break down the special sugar in milk. Originally, that's what happened in humans too.

But when some people started taming and keeping such animals as cows, goats and reindeer, they had a new source of milk. Most still couldn't drink milk straight without getting upset stomachs or diarrhea because they couldn't digest the milk sugar. So they used milk to make cheese or yogurt, in which milk sugar is already broken down.

For some reason, a few groups of people—mostly in northern Europe and a few places in Africa—never lost the enzymes needed to digest milk sugar. They became milk drinkers as well as eating cheese and other milk products. When these people settled in North America, they brought their dairy animals with them.

The Chinese and others such as the native people of North America had no milk animals. So their diets had no dairy products, and they didn't develop their ability to digest milk.

Nowadays, specially treated milk is available for people who have trouble digesting milk sugar so they can get the benefit of all the vitamins and minerals milk has to offer. And most countries have some dairy animals. Even China is starting a small dairy industry. So maybe someday, you will find Chinese cheese.

PLANTING AN IDEA

How many plants have you eaten in the past week? 10? 30? 100? 200? (Don't forget to count the "hidden" plants like the grains in bread and crackers.)

If you're like everyone else, you probably ate about 30.

From 300 000 to 100

There are about 300 000 plants in the world, but only about 30 000 are known to be edible by people. And only a hundred or so are actually grown and eaten on a regular basis somewhere in the world.

Why do people eat so few? We eat the hundred plants that were first domesticated early in history. Other plants were harder to grow, so people didn't bother with them. Instead they stuck with the first easy-to-grow hundred. Why experiment when you have something that works?

30 favourites

Out of the hundred plants that are commonly eaten, people in any part of the world usually eat only about 30. Why?

The main reason is that people mostly eat the plants that grow easily where they live. Of course, with modern transportation and storage, people have more variety available today. Food can be brought from all over the world to your local grocery store so you no longer have to eat just what is grown nearby. But still, local customs frequently determine what people eat.

The Big Four

The four plants you eat most are probably wheat, rice, corn and potatoes. They provide more than half of the world's food from plants. More than one-third of the people in the world use wheat as a staple (main) food and one-third use rice.

How did these four plants become so popular? Years ago, people experimented with different plants. They discovered that wheat, rice, corn and potatoes

were the most nutritious. They were also easy to grow, travelled well and produced the greatest amount of food.

People don't always choose the most nutritious plants as the main part of their diets. In Africa, many people grow and eat a root vegetable called cassava. It's not especially nutritious. In fact, many people are malnourished because cassava is the main part of their diet. It's still used a lot, though, because it's easy to grow, even in poor soil.

TRY THIS

Count the plants

Keep a list of all the different plants you eat in a week. See if you can eat twice as many different plants next week. Ask a friend whose family is from a different culture to do the same and compare your lists.

45

THAT SINKING FEELING

I F you think of food as packages of vitamins, proteins and nutrients, think of fibre as the string that holds all those packages together.

Fibre, also called roughage, is really non-food food—it's food that your stomach can't digest. You get it from whole grain breads and cereals, fruits and vegetables and legumes (dried beans and peas).

If you don't digest it, why eat it? Because you still use it. Fibre passes through your body quickly and acts like a neighbourhood garbage truck. It picks up waste in your intestines and carries it out through your bowels.

Get enough fibre and going to the bathroom is a lot easier. Fibre adds bulk to your stool. It also holds water. People who get plenty of fibre in their diets produce floaters. Their stool is big, soft and bulky and passes quickly. But if you don't eat enough fibre you produce sinkers—small, hard stools that are difficult and, at times, even painful to pass.

Nutritionists recommend you get between 28 and 40 g of fibre a day. A balanced diet including wide selection from all the food groups (dairy, meat, vegetable and fruit, bread and cereal) is the best way to guarantee your body gets what it needs.

Try this
Fibre test
Can you guess which foods in this list have the most fibre and which ones have the least? Number them from 1 to 8. Number 1 is the food with the most fibre; number 8 is the food with the least fibre. (Answers on page 91.)

1 slice whole-wheat bread
1 slice white bread
1 apple
16 grapes
1 egg
1 raw carrot
2 shredded wheat biscuits
125 mL (½ cup) baked beans

SINKER... OR FLOATER? THAT IS THE QUESTION

TALE OF TWO RATS

WHAT would you look like if you ate all the junk food you wanted? Probably a lot like Leon the rat.

Leon and his friend Harry grew up together. There the similarities ended.

Leon was raised in what seemed like paradise. Fat was mixed with his regular food so that his diet was like a human's who eats lots of french fries, fried chicken and other fried food. He had all the "goodies" anyone could want—sweetened milk and water, hot dogs, snacks of cookies, chocolate bars and potato chips.

Leon never exercised, either. He spent all his free time waiting around his cage for yet another yummy handout.

The result? Leon was one fat rat.

Old buddy Harry was another story entirely. Harry only chowed down on nutritious food with little fat. What's more, he drank only water. His favourite pastime was putting in a few laps on his exercise wheel.

He was one rat in tip top shape.

Besides being too fat to do much or enjoy life, Leon was eating foods that were dangerous for him—the same way that diets like his are dangerous for humans. Eating lots of fat and food with little nutrition in it can lead to big health problems, including heart disease.

Like rats, you need a balanced diet. Junk food may sound pretty good but what your body really craves is not just another potato chip but selections from the four food groups: dairy, fruits and vegetables, grains and meat. You need them all for your body to grow strong and healthy. Exercise helps to keep it that way.

Just like Harry the rat.

47

A DETECTIVE STORY

YOU'VE heard of private eyes? Well, I'm a private mouth. I solve food mysteries for people. That's why they call me Taster.

I remember one case. I was sitting in my office, my feet on my desk. I was reading a comic book. The cops walked in.

"Taster," they pleaded. "You've got to help us. Salt and sugar are on the loose again and we don't know where to find them. They're two of the most common ingredients found in food, but they're wearing disguises. We tried tasting the food, but we just aren't sure. Will you take the case?"

Salt and sugar on the loose. It sounded like a case I could get my tongue around. Sounded pretty simple too. Find a couple of hidden ingredients.

I was dead wrong.

I went with the police down to the station. The long tongue of the law had lapped up quite a list of suspects, a real shopping list.

They were in a line-up against the wall. They all looked innocent enough, but I knew somewhere in there the culprits were hiding.

Sure, I knew sugar and salt are two ingredients that nutritionists recommend you cut down on for your health. And I knew why. Sugar contains only calories. It promises a lot, but doesn't deliver—except maybe as cavities in your teeth or by making you fat. Yeah, it tastes good, but it doesn't give your body any vitamins, minerals, proteins or anything else it needs to live or stay healthy.

Salt is almost as bad. Your body needs salt to live, but eating too much can cause problems, especially if you have high blood pressure.

So there they were.

I knew it was going to shock the chief of police. She was an old friend and I hated to break it to her.

"Chief," I said under my breath, "I've got news for you. All of them are guilty. You can't always be sure

TRY THIS

Can you solve these food mysteries?

How good are your food detective powers? Try these two tests and then turn to page 91 for the answers.

1. Which has the most salt:
   250 mL (1 c) of instant chocolate pudding
   250 mL (1 c) of salted peanuts
   250 mL (1 c) of O-shaped oat cereal
2. Which has the most sugar:
   250 mL (1 c) of cola
   250 mL (1 c) of ketchup
   250 mL (1 c) of flavoured yogurt

by taste alone. If you read the ingredients on the label you'd have known they've all got sugar or salt in them."

The chief seemed surprised.

"But we read the labels," she said.

"Look here," I told her, pointing to the ingredients. "Glucose, fructose, sucrose—all forms of sugar. And sodium chloride and monosodium glutamate, also known as MSG—they're forms of salt."

"I didn't know that," said the chief gratefully. "Thanks, Taster. We'll let them go this time, but we'll make sure we keep an eye on them and try to cut down wherever we can."

"All in a day's work," I said as I walked out the police station door. If I didn't love my work, I wouldn't do it.

After all, I'm a private mouth. I solve food mysteries for people. That's why they call me Taster.

NO FOOLING WITH FUELLING

Your body is like an engine. How energetically and how smoothly you chug along depends a lot on what and how much you chomp on.

While a car chugs along on gasoline, your body is fuelled by calories. But you have a lot more choices than regular, unleaded or super.

All food has calories—some more than others. Calories are a way of measuring the energy you get from the food you eat. In scientific terms, a calorie is the amount of heat you would need to raise the temperature of one kilogram of water one degree Celsius. Theoretically, if you set fire to a piece of food that had 5 calories in it, and heated a kilogram of water over the flame, the water would be $5°C$ hotter by the time the food finished burning.

In body terms, calories provide the energy you need for all your activities: breathing, walking, sleeping, playing ball. You even need energy to eat!

In a car, the fuel tank only holds so much gas. If you put in more fuel, it spills on the ground. But if you eat more than you need, your body keeps the extra calories. They're stored as fat. When your body needs more energy, you either give it more food or it uses your stored fat.

So why not just eat any food to get energy? A car runs best on the quality gasoline it was made to use. If you put regular gas in a car designed for super fuel, the car just won't run right. Your body runs best on the foods it was made for too. Poor quality food, with poor or no nutritional value leaves you chugging along at half speed.

Although all food has calories, you also need nutrients such as vitamins, minerals and proteins. Some foods have more of these nutrients than others. For example, you get about the same number of calories in a chocolate bar as you do in a piece of chicken—270. The chocolate bar is mostly calories. But the chicken has protein and other things your body needs to grow and stay healthy.

How full is full enough for your tank, er, stomach? The average 10 year old needs about 2300 calories a day. If you want your machine to run smoothly, fill it up with high-quality fuel—and away you'll go!

The chocolate bar workout

It takes you only a minute to eat a chocolate bar, but how long would you have to run to burn off the calories from that bar? About 14 minutes.

You could walk off the calories in 52 minutes or swim them off in 24.

Standing and singing burns almost 2 calories per minute. It would take a lot of verses of "99 Chocolate Bars On The Wall" to wear off your candy snack.

Of course, you could burn off your treat by watching TV, but it would take you 4 hours to use up the calories in one chocolate bar! Even sleeping uses calories—5 hours sleep would just about take care of that chocolate bar.

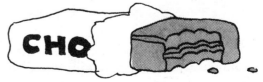

CHOOSE A MEAL

ICK one of these meals and see how healthy it is for you. Then turn to page 91 to see how well you did.

Meal A
two hot dogs in buns
french fries
cola

Meal B
lean roast beef
baked potato and a pat of butter
green beans
slice of chocolate cake
glass of milk

Meal C
omelet
corn on the cob with a pat of butter
french fries
cherry pie
milk

What's in a healthy meal?
A healthy meal should have a balance of:

Proteins, the building blocks you need for the growth and maintenance of your body. You get them from meat, dried beans, grains and vegetables.

Carbohydrates, your body's main source of energy. There are two kinds of carbohydrates: simple and complex. Simple carbohydrates are sugars. They're naturally found in foods like milk or fruit and are also added to foods such as candy, cake and ice cream.

Complex carbohydrates are starches and cellulose. They're found in food such as potatoes, bread, vegetables and rice.

Fats, a high-calorie source of energy. You also need them for growth and to keep your skin healthy. You find them in meats, nuts, cheese and milk.

In a well-balanced meal, you get about half of your calories from carbohydrates, a little more than a third of your calories from fat and the rest (about an eighth) from proteins.

What about vitamins and minerals?
Vitamins are chemicals that help your body function. A few of the important ones you need are:

- Vitamin A, for healthy skin, strong bones and good vision. It's in such foods as yellow, green and orange vegetables.
- B Vitamins for your nervous system, healthy skin and eyes and to help your body use protein, fat and carbohydrates. You get them from meats and whole grain breads.
- Vitamin C, to help make blood vessels, bones and teeth. It's found in fruits and leafy green vegetables.

Even though you don't need large amounts of minerals, they are necessary to build bones (calcium) and help cells do their work (iron) and for other essential body functions.

TRY THIS

Where's the fat

Nutritionists say it's not healthy to eat too much fat. But how can you tell if you're feasting on fat in a food?

You'll need:

a brown paper bag

several different kinds of foods—for instance, meat, french fries or potato chips, carrot, milk, apple juice

1. Cut the brown paper bag into about 7 cm (3 inch) squares. Label each square with the name of one of the foods you have.
2. Rub some of each food on the square with its name or, if it's a liquid, put a few drops on the square.
3. Let the squares dry.
4. When they're dry, hold each square up to a light. What effect did different foods have on the paper?

What's happening

The spots where light shines through the paper show that fat has been absorbed from the food you put on it.

Different substances let light pass through them at different speeds. Whenever light travels from one substance to another and changes speeds abruptly, some of it gets scattered. Paper is made of many strands of fibre, with air between them. Because light travels through air and fibre at very different speeds, most of the light gets scattered as it goes from air to fibre to air to fibre and very little gets through.

But light travels through fat and fibre at very similar speeds. When fat soaks into the air spaces between the fibres that make up the paper, light can pass through the paper without as much scattering, turning your brown paper squares into fat detectors.

INSIDE STORY OF A HOT DOG

THERE mustard be some secret ingredient in hot dogs that everyone relishes, because other foods just can't ketchup with their popularity. They're so enjoyable, so much bun to eat. But why do they call it a hot dog?

Just as there is no butter in peanut butter and no ham in hamburger, there's no dog in a hot dog. Disguised under the name of frankfurter, hot dogs were introduced to North America sometime in the late 1800s. No one's sure who first started selling the Frankfurt sausage, named after the city of Frankfurt, Germany. What we do know is that in 1906 a cartoonist named Tad drew a cartoon featuring a frankfurter with a dog's legs, head and tail. This odd looking dachshund was dubbed a hot dog and the name stuck.

Whether you call them weiners (another German name, meaning "from the city of Vienna"), frankfurters or hot dogs, they're all made the same way. Spices are added to ground meat—beef, pork, veal and sometimes chicken or turkey. Then it's squeezed through a tiny hole—much like the way you squeeze toothpaste out of a tube—and into a casing (a hot-dog-shaped bag). The process of forcing something through a small hole so that it will take on a certain shape is called extrusion. It's used for lots of foods besides hot dogs—sausages, cheese puffs, pasta and many breakfast cereals. It's even used for some plastic toys!

After the hot dogs are smoked for one to three hours, they're cooked by spraying them with hot water. Finally, they're put in cold water and the casing is taken off. But even without its casing, a hot dog—like a banana—still has appeal.

THE WHEAT GAME

BEING a farmer has to be one of the world's greatest jobs! You're outside in the sunshine all day, riding around on your tractor, wearing your most comfortable clothes. You grow your own food, so you don't have to worry about going to the store. As far as growing food is concerned, what could be easier? All you have to do is plant a seed and watch it grow. Right? Not quite.

To give you a better sense of what farming is really like, try playing The Wheat Game on the next page.

Wheat is the world's largest crop. One-seventh of all farm land around the world is used for growing wheat. Every moment of the year some farmer, somewhere, is harvesting wheat, and another one is planting it.

Here's your chance to see what farming is really like, and you don't even have to get dirty—or develop any blisters.

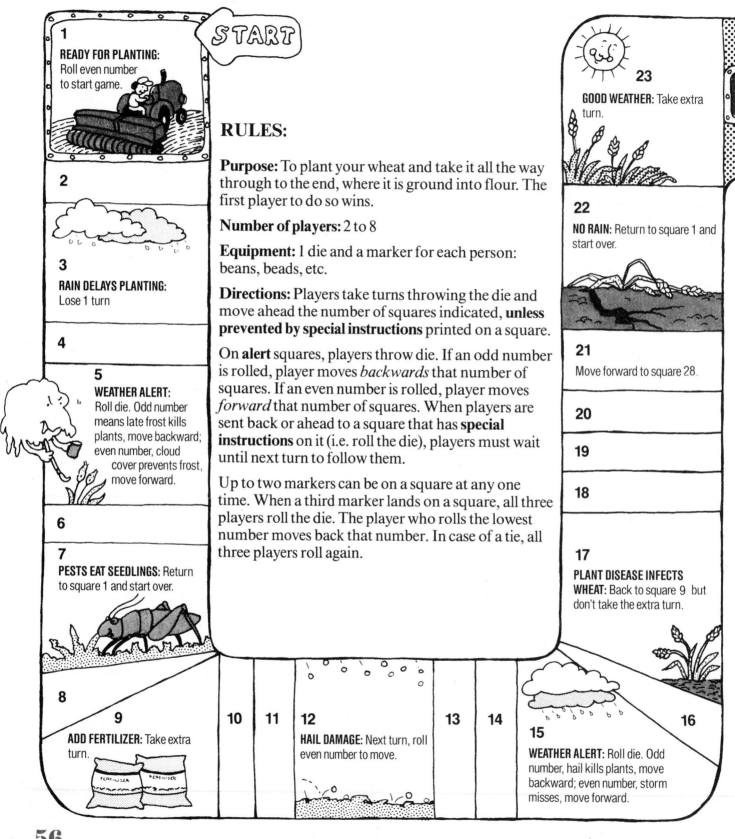

START

1
READY FOR PLANTING:
Roll even number to start game.

2

3
RAIN DELAYS PLANTING:
Lose 1 turn

4

5
WEATHER ALERT:
Roll die. Odd number means late frost kills plants, move backward; even number, cloud cover prevents frost, move forward.

6

7
PESTS EAT SEEDLINGS: Return to square 1 and start over.

8

9
ADD FERTILIZER: Take extra turn.

10

11

12
HAIL DAMAGE: Next turn, roll even number to move.

13

14

15
WEATHER ALERT: Roll die. Odd number, hail kills plants, move backward; even number, storm misses, move forward.

16

17
PLANT DISEASE INFECTS WHEAT: Back to square 9 but don't take the extra turn.

18

19

20

21
Move forward to square 28.

22
NO RAIN: Return to square 1 and start over.

23
GOOD WEATHER: Take extra turn.

RULES:

Purpose: To plant your wheat and take it all the way through to the end, where it is ground into flour. The first player to do so wins.

Number of players: 2 to 8

Equipment: 1 die and a marker for each person: beans, beads, etc.

Directions: Players take turns throwing the die and move ahead the number of squares indicated, **unless prevented by special instructions** printed on a square.

On **alert** squares, players throw die. If an odd number is rolled, player moves *backwards* that number of squares. If an even number is rolled, player moves *forward* that number of squares. When players are sent back or ahead to a square that has **special instructions** on it (i.e. roll the die), players must wait until next turn to follow them.

Up to two markers can be on a square at any one time. When a third marker lands on a square, all three players roll the die. The player who rolls the lowest number moves back that number. In case of a tie, all three players roll again.

24 RAIN DELAY: Too much rain slows growth. Next turn, roll even number to move.

25

26 PEST ALERT: Roll die. Odd number, many locusts eat crop, move backward; even number, few locusts, little damage, move forward.

WARNING

27

28 WEATHER ALERT: Roll die. Odd number, heat damages plants, move backward; even number, good rainfall, move forward.

29

30 PLANT DISEASE: Wheat turns black. Back to square 9 , but don't take the extra turn.

31 ORGANIZE HARVEST: Lose 1 turn.

Fix combine ✓
oil auger ✓
repair bins ✓
order parts
for tractor

35 EXTRA FARM HANDS HIRED: Ahead 4.

34 RAIN DELAY: Fields too muddy to harvest. Next turn must roll even number to move.

33

32 EQUIPMENT ALERT: Roll die. Odd number, tractor broken, move backward; even number, tractor repaired, move forward.

36

37 FARM HAND QUITS: Back 1.

44

45

46 RAIL STRIKE: Lose 1 turn.

47 BUYER CANCELS ORDER: Back to 40

RATS INFEST STORAGE SHED: Lose 1 turn.

48 SHIPPING DELAY: Must roll even number to move.

38 FIRE DESTROYS CROP: Start over.

43 EQUIPMENT ALERT: Roll die. Odd number, you can't afford new truck to ship grain, move backward; even number, you can buy truck, move forward.

49

50 WHEAT GROUND INTO FLOUR: Game over.

39

40 PREPARE TO MEET BUYER: Lose 1 turn.

41 SELLING ALERT: Roll die. Odd number, price too low, move backward; even number, good price, move forward.

42

FINISH

FLOUR FLOUR FLOUR FLOUR FLOUR FLOUR

A DIRTY STORY

YOU may think the stuff that you wash off your hands is the very same stuff that plants can't live without—dirt. But you're only partly right.

Actually, dirt is almost useless to a plant. It's only finely ground rocks and minerals. What plants need is *soil*. Soil is dirt with character.

To get soil you mix dirt with decayed plants and animals (decomposed organic matter), air and water. The organic matter gives plants about 10 per cent of their nourishment. The rest comes from the atmosphere.

Who cares about the difference between dirt and soil? Plants do! Most plants can't thrive in dirt with a lot of coarse sand, gravel or stone. It just won't hold the nutrients and water they need to survive. Soil that contains a lot of clay, however, *will* hold these things, and plants thrive like Jack's magic beanstalk.

What else does soil contain that plants need? If you could scoop up half a hectare (an acre) of typical farm soil down to a depth of 15 cm (6 inches), you'd find:

- 1-2 tonnes (tons) of fungi—organisms that live on dead matter
- 1-2 tonnes (tons) of bacteria—creatures that have only a single cell
- 90 kg (200 pounds) of one-celled animals called protozoa
- 45 kg (100 pounds) of tiny water plants called algae
- 45 kg (100 pounds) of yeasts, which are microscopic plant/animals.

These help break down the organic matter in soil so the plants can pull the nutrients out of it.

How thick is the soil on Earth? Think of the world as a tomato. The skin of the tomato compared to its size is much, much thicker than the layer of soil covering the Earth compared to its size.

That sounds like a pretty thin layer of soil—and it is. Because it is so thin, loss of topsoil, or "erosion," is a major problem in the world. It's estimated that 75 billion tonnes (tons) of soil are lost in the world every year—just about 1 per cent of all the topsoil there is.

When good soil rich in nutrients is blown away by wind or washed away by heavy rains, it eventually ends up in the ocean where it stays forever. It can take from 100 to 2500 years for the natural wearing down of rocks and collection of nutrients to make 2.5 cm (1 inch) of topsoil. It only takes 10 years to lose it. If too much soil is lost, all that's left is a desert.

Erosion can be controlled by taking care of the soil. Plants help anchor soil in place. Their roots help hold the topsoil down so that it can't blow or wash away. With some care in planting and by keeping forests from being cut down or marshes from being drained, the harmful effects of erosion can be reduced.

TRY THIS

A dirty job

In nature, it takes hundreds of years to make soil. You can make your own in just a matter of minutes. The trick? You can use a hammer: nature can't.

You'll need:
cheesecloth or an old cotton tea towel
very small stones (limestone or sandstone work best) or a brick (not asphalt—it contains petroleum products and will not work for this experiment)
a hammer
peat moss (buy at a hardware store or garden centre)
plant leftovers (cut-up fruit or vegetable skins, tea leaves, coffee grounds)
broken or crushed eggshells
water

1. Completely wrap the rocks in the cheesecloth or tea towel.
2. Pound and pound and pound the rocks with the hammer until they're smashed into tiny bits about the size of a grain of sugar. It will take you about 5 to 10 minutes of pounding.
3. Once the rocks are pulverized, add an equal amount of peat moss to them. (Or use half sand and half peat moss.) Peat moss conditions the soil and helps it to hold water.
4. Add the plant leftovers and broken eggshells.
5. Add some water and mix it all together.
   Is this really soil? To find out, see if a plant will grow in it. Put the mixture in a jar and plant a bean seed in it. Leave it in the sun and keep it moist. Does it grow?

THE SECRET LIFE OF SEEDS

WHAT do peas, rice, peanuts, corn, beans, wheat and nuts have in common? Besides the fact that you eat them, they're all seeds.

Seeds are more than just a way to grow food: many seeds actually are food themselves! For example, some seeds are used to season food, such as anise, caraway, coriander, dill, pepper and celery seeds. Others, like corn and peanuts, are squeezed to make oil. Still others make great snacks when roasted—for example, pumpkin and sunflower seeds.

Although they don't have legs to help them get around, aren't clever like some animals and can't fight off predators, seeds have talents few people notice.

Most seeds (except an impatient few) are able to wait for exactly the right moment before germinating, or beginning to grow. This can mean a wait of one year, ten years, even 85 years. Seeds found after several thousand years in the tombs of Egyptian pharaohs or kings were still able to germinate!

This talent means that a seed can wait for everything to be just right—water, temperature, light, oxygen—before taking the big plunge and sending out a shoot.

A lot of things can set a seed off sprouting. Most seeds germinate after a dormant, or inactive, period.

Some seeds' growth is triggered by light. Some will grow only after a certain amount of rain. This is helpful in desert areas. Since plants need water to survive, sprouting after a lot of rain at least gives them a good start.

Other seeds, such as those from some water plants, are dormant until freezing and thawing cracks their outer coating or water wears it away. Still others, such as jack pine, germinate only after being exposed to extreme heat. These seeds are the first to sprout after a forest fire, bringing the forest back to life.

A lot of seeds grow only after being exposed to a cold spell. This keeps the plant from sprouting in the summer or fall when it wouldn't have a long enough season to grow.

Without legs, seeds have to be ingenious to get around. Animals and birds often unknowingly help seeds spread. For example, when squirrels store nuts for future meals, they sometimes forget where they bury them, leaving a trail of trees and plants to mark their absent-mindedness. When birds eat berries, they can't digest the seeds and excrete them after flying far away from the original plant.

Some seeds are "hitchhikers." They have small hooks or barbs to attach themselves to any animal—

including you—that comes by. They get carried off to other locations and dropped there.

"Parachuters," such as dandelions, and "winged" seeds, such as those from maple trees, are so light that they are blown easily from place to place.

"Shooting" seeds are formed in pods which burst open and fire them out.

Seed bank

You won't find any tellers in a seed bank. Instead you'll find seeds from thousands of different plants stored on temperature-controlled shelves.

Why are seeds "banked?" Many countries store seeds in seed banks in case an agricultural disease or some other disaster wipes out or threatens certain plants. Seeds are also saved in case anyone ever wants to use an old strain that's no longer being grown.

Of course, seeds can't be stored forever. When they start to get old they are planted so new seeds can be produced and saved.

TRY THIS

Seed stroll

Here's a simple way to collect seeds. Put an old pair of wool socks over your shoes and walk through a vacant lot or woods. Hitchhiking seeds will hang on to you just like they do on an animal's coat. You can pick them off with tweezers later to study them.

DIRTLESS FARMING

ow do you grow a garden without lots of good dirty dirt? With hydroponics. Its name tells you its secret. It comes from *hydro*, the Greek word for water, and *ponos*, the Greek word for labour—letting water do the work of soil. With your help, of course.

TRY THIS

Make your own hydroponic garden

You'll need:

a jar with a wide mouth

a plastic flower pot, styrofoam cup or other container that can rest just inside the mouth of the jar without falling in

a piece of cotton rope long enough to reach the bottom of the jar and up into the pot as shown

seeds—radish, lettuce, spinach, peas or green beans work best

vermiculite (granite that has been expanded under pressure. Available at garden centres)

plant nutrient (called hydroponic fertilizer. Available at garden centres)

1. Fray both ends of the rope. This is your "wick."
2. Put the rope through the bottom of your flower pot or other container so that it comes about 2/3 of the way up the container and the rest hangs down below. Hold it there while you fill the pot with vermiculite.
3. Make the plant nutrient by mixing the hydroponic fertilizer with water. Read the package directions to find out how much water to add.
4. Put enough nutrient into the jar so that when you sit the flower pot in the jar mouth, the liquid isn't touching the pot.
5. Sit the pot on the jar, letting the wick hang into the nutrient solution.
6. Plant your seeds in the vermiculite. Not too deep! Depending on the plant you have chosen and the size of your pot, you can plant two or three seeds in the pot. Just make sure the planting spots are 7-8 cm (about 3 inches) apart. It's a good idea to put two seeds at each spot, to make sure you get a sprout.
7. Put your vegetable garden in a window that gets a lot of sun every day. Make sure there's always enough nutrient solution in the jar to keep the wick wet. Plain water won't work: your plants will starve without the nutrients in the fertilizer.

Now watch it grow! Even though you haven't used soil, your seeds should sprout up in two to three weeks. If they're too crowded, pull out a few of the plants so they have 5-7 cm (about 2 inches) between them. Soon you'll be eating food from your own garden.

How does it work?

Soil provides *support* for the plants and *food* for them to grow. You've used vermiculite to support the plants and substituted fertilizer for the food they'd normally get from the decayed plants and animals in soil.

The wick, with its frayed ends, creates a kind of highway for the food and water to travel up to the plant's root area. With all these things, plus lots of sun, you've created an ideal environment for your plants.

Hydroponics then and now

Hydroponics isn't a new idea. It was used in the Hanging Gardens of Babylon thousands of years ago. The ancient Aztecs and the Chinese also used hydroponics.

Today many hydroponic greenhouses grow vegetables year-round in areas where seasonal changes make it impossible to grow them in the ground. Restaurants frequently serve hydroponically grown vegetables, particularly lettuce. Not only is it available locally and fresh all the time, but it's clean too. (Vermiculite doesn't stick to plants the way soil does.) And since the plants are being grown in a controlled environment, they're also free of insects and insecticides.

The only thing that's wrong with hydroponic gardening is that it doesn't give you a good excuse to get your hands dirty!

OLD MACDONALD HAD SOME FISH

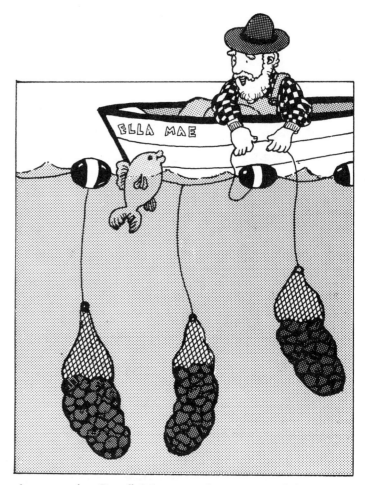

WHAT could you grow in socks—besides toe-matoes? How about fish? Farmers are beginning to realize that they are not limited to raising two- and four-legged animals that make a lot of noise. They are getting into the swim of things and breeding and harvesting fish. Farming fish or plants in water is known as aquaculture.

Mussels, a type of mollusk, something like a clam, normally grow wild in the ocean. Anyone who wants to catch them has to find them first. Instead of going to all that trouble, fish farmers grow them in special nylon "socks" which they hang from buoy lines in protected ocean coves.

Raising mussels in this way has a lot of advantages. You don't have to go hunting for them—they're exactly where you left them. And if any of the mussels are diseased, it's easy to find and remove them before they infect the others. Finally, mussels in socks are safer from their enemies—natural predators and sand.

You wouldn't think of sand as a problem for an animal that lives in the ocean, but it is. As with oysters and clams, if sand gets inside a mussel, it irritates it. To protect itself, the mussel covers the sand with a solution which becomes a pearl. Finding a pearl isn't always as great as it sounds, however. Most pearls formed in mussels and oysters aren't valuable. Besides, how would you enjoy chewing a nice tender mussel, only to find a rock got there first!

Farmers in Hawaii grow oysters but instead of socks, they use trays and nets.

Fish are being raised in other places besides the ocean. They may soon be farmed in silos right in the middle of large cities. Fish silos are just what they sound like—small cylinders that look like the silos you see on farms, except that they are filled with water and packed with fish, such as trout and salmon. Water flows over the fish constantly and they keep swimming to fight the current. Fish farmers have found that their "crop" tastes better as a result of all that exercise. But fish have to sleep too, and they need calm water to sleep in, so the farmer has to shut the pump down at night. The farmer doesn't have to feed the fish in a silo. They feed themselves. Whenever they're hungry, the fish push a rod, which releases food into the water.

Fish farmers have to watch a lot of other things when they're packing them in like sardines, though. For instance, fish can't live in a toilet. To keep things clean the silos have a double filter system. One filter cleans out the large particles of fish waste. The other has bacteria in it which break down the remainder.

These filters make it possible to recycle 80-90 per cent of the water in the silo. This means you don't have to be near a constant source of water, such as a lake in the country. You can raise finny friends right in the middle of the city.

TRY THIS

Light up

Although you don't have to shovel out the fish barn, you do have to keep other things in mind to raise fish, such as where the light comes from. What difference can the direction of light make? You can find out by trying this test.

You'll need:
a flashlight
a glass goldfish bowl with goldfish living in it
a friend to help

1. Make the room as dark as possible.
2. Shine a flashlight on top of the water in your gold-fish bowl. Do the fish still swim normally?
3. Shine the light on the side of the bowl for about 15 minutes. What happens to the way the fish are swimming?
4. (WARNING! DON'T DO THIS STEP FOR LONGER THAN HALF AN HOUR OR YOU COULD HARM YOUR FISH.) Have a friend carefully hold the bowl (or put it on a glass table) and shine the light up from the bottom. What do the fish do?

Warm up

Fish need more than food to grow. Temperature can make a difference. You can find out how different temperatures affect fish with this longer experiment.

You'll need:
2 goldfish of the same size
2 aquariums or goldfish bowls
2 thermometers
2 aquarium heaters (optional)

1. Set up the two aquariums with one fish each.
2. Keep one aquarium warm, about 30°C (86°F), by putting it in a warm place or installing an aquarium heater.
3. Keep the other aquarium relatively cold, about 18-20°C (65-68°F).

Which fish is larger at the end of the month? If you were a fish farmer, how would you regulate the water temperature to make your fish grow faster?

A COMPUTER THAT GOES MOO

I F you become a farmer, you're just as likely to have calloused fingers from typing on your computer as you are from pitching hay. Instead of a tractor, you could be riding a computer terminal most of the day.

Researchers are experimenting right now with implanting small computers in the necks of cows and other animals to help keep track of them. When the farmer wants to know where his cows are, a central computer will put a map of his farm on the screen and pinpoint where every cow is by "reading" their neck computers.

Computers are already being used to monitor cows' health. They even keep track of feedings. When a computerized cow goes to the computerized barn it touches its nose to a metal plate on the wall. The barn's computer then knows which cow it's feeding, and just what and how much to feed it.

By carefully breeding from selected cows and bulls, farmers today have produced super cows. These specially bred animals grow more quickly and give more milk than ordinary cows. Super chickens grow more quickly too. They also start laying eggs earlier, lay more of them and for a longer time. In the future, genetic engineering may produce new breeds of animals that are even more super.

There are not only better animals, there are new animal foods too. Cow nutritionists have developed a new diet consisting of sawdust mixed with tomato juice, tomato pulp, yeast and the stillage, or waste, from a whiskey distillery. This yummy mixture not only produces healthy animals, but is very cheap, since it uses material that would otherwise be thrown away.

There is more to a farm than just animals. In future, crops such as wheat and corn will also be taken care of by computer. These crop computers will regulate watering, determine the proper time to plant and harvest, monitor insects and soil conditions and run

the automated equipment that will do the actual work.

Much of that work will be done by computer-controlled robots. Farm equipment companies are already working on tractors and other equipment that can be programmed to plow a field, plant seeds, spray and harvest all by themselves.

And what will you be doing, if you don't have to be out in the fields or in the barn feeding your animals? Well, you'll spend a lot more time riding your computer.

Past and future farmers

Besides making farming easier, computers will make it more productive. In the year 1700, when most of a farmer's tools were at the end of a stick, the average farm worker grew enough food to feed three people.

Things got better slowly. In 1860, a farm worker could grow enough for five people. By 1902, this had climbed to 15 people. With modern machinery, in 1952, it was 50 people. Today it's 80, and by the year 2000, thanks to the use of computer technology, genetic engineering and new farming methods, a single farm worker will be able to grow enough food to feed a hundred people.

MANMADE PLANTS AND ANIMALS

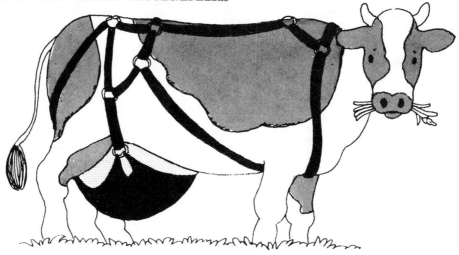

WHAT do you get when you cross a carrot with a kangaroo? A snack that fits inside its own pocket!

Maybe crossing a carrot with a kangaroo sounds farfetched to you, but it just might be possible some day. Researchers are trying to cross all sorts of plants and animals in different ways. They've come up with some interesting results.

For thousands of years, **selective breeding** has been the way that people developed different types of plants and animals. You start by selecting the characteristics of the plant or animal you want to produce—dogs with long hair, for instance, or tulips that grow tall. You choose the longest-haired dogs and the tallest tulips you can find to breed from. From the next generation, you choose the hairiest or tallest to breed from again and you carry on this way for several generations, until you have dogs that need hair nets or tulips that can see over all the other plants.

Through this kind of selective breeding, a new breed of cow has been developed with a greatly enlarged udder. It produces a lot more milk than the average cow. One problem, though. The udder is so large, the cow needs to wear a "bra" to support it.

Bigger and better isn't just limited to farm animals, either. By using **genetic engineering** to insert human growth hormone genes into developing mice, scientists have produced mice that are the size of rats. If they continue, will there soon be goose-sized chickens and elephant-sized cows?

Scientists are also trying to create plants that are more resistant to disease and cold. If you can grow a plant that a disease will not harm, you don't have to spray chemicals on it to cure the disease—chemicals which might be harmful to humans or other animals and plants.

Faster growing plants are also being developed. With fast growing plants, more crops can be grown in a shorter time. That means more food can be produced for more people. And trees that normally would take 80 years to grow large enough to use as wood could reach maturity in half that time.

A lot of this is done by **cross-fertilization** of related plants—putting pollen from one plant on the flowers of another. A cross between a potato and a tomato has been grown this way—but it tastes terrible. Scientists have also crossed a bean and a sunflower, creating a sunbean. Sunflowers produce lots of oil and protein in their seeds; beans don't need much fertilizer because their roots produce nitrogen. A sunbean could be a very valuable plant.

The possibilities for new plants and animals seem endless. Scientists have even managed to put human genes in a petunia plant.

You may not ever have a snack that fits inside its own pocket, but how about wheat that drives itself to the flour mill or maybe corn that pops itself?

GUESS THE FOOD

PACKAGED foods are like surprise packages—you can't tell what's in them just by looking. Many unexpected ingredients go into apparently simple manufactured foods. Some of those ingredients—about 4 kg (8.8 pounds) of the food you eat in one year—are chemical additives put in by manufacturers. They're there for a lot of reasons—to preserve freshness, help the ingredients mix together better, add flavour and colour and more.

With all those additives and other ingredients in packaged food, it's sometimes difficult to know exactly what you're eating. For example, look at these five lists of ingredients. Can you guess what foods they make up? Answers on page 91.

1.
Ingredient	Purpose
Tomatoes	Main ingredient. Gives flavour, texture and colour
Sugar	Flavour and preservation
High fructose corn syrup	Flavour and sweetness
Vinegar	Preserves and gives sour flavour
Salt	Flavour
Spice concentrate	Flavour

2.
Ingredient	Purpose
Glucose	For sweetness and smooth texture
Sugar	Sweetness
Water	Mixes ingredients and adds moisture
Corn starch	Makes it firm and dough like
Gelatin	Helps make it fluffy and tender
Tetrasodium pyrophosphate	Helps in whipping it

Artificial flavour	Vanilla, vanillin (made from wood products) and propylene glycol—all for flavour

3.

Ingredient	Purpose
Gum base	Main ingredient. Made of natural or synthetic gum, pine tree rosin, filler, emulsifier, plasticizers, wax
Mannitol	Sweetness, body and to retain moisture
Glycerine	Texture, body and to retain moisture and keep it soft
Natural or artificial flavour	Flavour
Lecithin	From soybeans. Helps it stay mixed
Aspartame	Artificial sweetener
Beta-carotene	Colour
Calcium carbonate	A type of limestone. Keeps it from sticking

4.

Ingredient	Purpose
Sugar	Flavour and sweetness
Glucose	Type of sugar, for flavour and sweetness
Modified starch	Used as binder to hold product together
Liquid invert sugar	Sweetness and to make it moist
Icing sugar	Flavour and sweetness
Carnauba wax	To give it a sheen
Mineral oil	Keep it from sticking to itself
Artificial flavour and colour	Flavour and to make it look good

5. Not everything in the food you eat is added by a manufacturer. These compounds are all found naturally in one additive-free food that you probably eat often.

Alanine, gamma-Aminobutyric Acid, Arginine, Aspargine, Aspartic acid, Cystine, Glutamic acid, Glycine, Histidine, Isoleucine, Allo-Isoleucine Leucine, Lysine, Methionine, Phenyl-alanine, Proline, Serine, Threonine Tyrosine, Valine, Betaine, Synephrine, Phytoene, Phytofluene, delta-Carotene, alpha-Carotene, 3-hydroxy-alpha-Carotene, Cryptoxanthin, 3-hydroxy-5, 6-epoxy-alpha-Carotene, 3-hydroxy-5, 8-epoxypalpha-Carotene, 5,6-epoxycryptoxanthin, Crypto-flavinlike, 5,6,5',6'-diepoxycryptoxanthin, 5,6,5',8'-diepoxycryptoxanthin, Zeaxanthin, Lutein, 5,6-epoxylutein, Flavoxanthin, Antheraxanthin, Mutatoxanthin, Violaxanthin, Luteoxanthin, Auroxanthin, Neoxanthin, Trollixanthin, Trollichrome, Trolliflor, Hesperidan: 3',5,7-trihydroxy-4'-methoxyflavonan, Aconitic acid, Adipic acid, Benzoic acid, Chlorogenic acid, Citramalic acid, Citric acid, Galacturonic acid, Isocitric acid, lactic acid, Malic acid, Malonic acid, Oxalic acid, Phosphonic acid, Quinic acid, Succinic acid, Tartaric acid, Cyanidin-3-glucoside, delphinidin-3-glucoside, beta-sitosterol-betaD-glucoside, gamma-sitosterol-betaD-glucoside, cholesterol-betaD-glucoside, Phlorin, Furuloylputreseine, Sinensiaxanthin, Sinensiachrome, Valenciachrome, Valenciachrome, Hesperidin: 3'5,7-trihydroxy-4'-methoxyflavanone-7-rutinoside, Naringenin: 4'5,7-tetrahydroxyflavone, Isosakuranetin: 5,7-dihydroxy-4'-methoxyflavone, Nobiletin: 3',4',5,6,7,8-hexamethoxyflavone, Tangeretin: 4,5,6,7,8-pentamethoxyflavone: 5,8-dihydroxy-3,3',4,7-tetramethoxyflavone; 3',4',5,6,7-pentamethoxy flavone, Tetra-o-methyl scutellarein, Limetin: 5,7-dimethoxy coumarin, Bergoptol: 5-hydroxpsoralen, Aurapten: 7-geranoxy coumarin, Isoimperatorin: 5(2'-isopentenoxy)-psoralen, Meranzin: 7-methoxy-8 (2',3'-dihydroxy isopentoxy)-psoralen, Limonin: 8-(3-furyl)-decahydro-2,2,4alpha, 8alpha-tetramethyl-11H, 13H-Oxireno-(d)-larano-(4',3':3, 3alpha)-isobenzofuro-(5,4f)-(2)-benzopyran-4,6,13-(2H, 5alphaH)-trione, Obacunone, Ascorbic Acid, Biotin, Choline, Folic Acid, Inositol, Nicotinic Acid, Pantothenic Acid, Pyridoxine, Riboflavin, Thiamine, Citraurin, Reticulataxanthin, alpha-Pinene, beta-Pinene, Camphene, Sabinene, alpha-Thujene, delta-3-Carene, Myrcene, Limonene, alpha - Phellandrene, isoterpinolene, Terpinolene, gamma-Terpinene, beta-Terpinene, Alpha-Terpinene, p.Cymene, Farnesene, alpha-Ylangene, beta-Ylangene, beta-Bisabolene, alpha-Bergamotene, delta-Cadinene, gamma-Cadinene, alpha-Cubebene, beta-Cubebene, alpha-Copaene, beta-Copaene, beta-Elemene, Valencene, alpha-Humulene, beta-Caryophyllene, Longifolene, Methanol, Ethanol, 3-methyl Butanol, l-penten-3-ol, n.hexanol, n.octanol, 3-octanol, n.nonanol, n.decanol, n.undecanol, n.dodecanol, geraniol, Nerol, linalool, citronellol, thymol, alpha-terpineol, terpinen-4-ol, isopulegol, p-mentha-2,8-dien-l-ol, carveol, acetaldehyde, butanal, hexanal, 2-hexenal, heptanal, octanal, 2-octenal, nonanal, decanal, undecanal, dodecanal, benzaldehyde, furfuraldehyde, geranial, neral, citonellal, alpha-sinesal, beta-sinesal, cuminaldehyde, perillaldehyde, acetone, methyl heptanone, methyl heptenone, 6-methyl-5hepten-2-one, menthone, piperitenone, carvone, camphor, nootkatone, 1,1-diethoxy-ethane, 1,8-cineol, limonene oxide, octyl acetate, nonyl acetate, dodecyl acetate, decyl acetate, benzyl acetate, methyl butyrate, ethyl butyrate, ethyl 3-hydroxyhexanoate, geranyl acetate, neryl formate, neryl acetate, linalyl acetate, citronellyl acetate, perillyl acetate, p-mentha-1, 8-dien-9-yl acetate, methyl N-methyl anthranilate, butyric acid, octanoic acid, citronellic acid, 3-hydroxy hexanoic acid, enanthic acid, pelargonic acid.

I SCREAM, YOU SCREAM, WE ALL SCREAM FOR ICE CREAM

YOU may have heard that Marco Polo brought ice cream back to Europe when he went to China in 1295. Well, he didn't. He ate it all on the way. Luckily, though, Marco did bring back the recipe. That original recipe didn't have cream in it. It was a water ice, made with fruit juice, sugar and water, the same way ices are made today. Cream didn't get into the recipe until 300 years later in France.

You can guess some of the major ingredients in ice cream—cream, milk, sugar, flavouring—but you'd probably never think of one of the most important ones—plain, unflavoured, uncoloured *air*.

Air is stirred into ice cream as it freezes. Without air, eating ice cream would be like chewing milky ice cubes. But you can have too much of a good thing. The more air ice cream has, the fluffier and warmer it seems (warmer because it contains less of the ice and icy liquid that make you feel the coldness). Some ice creams, usually the cheaper varieties, have as much air in them as all the other ingredients put together.

For most of its history, ice cream was home made in a bucket or other container and the stirring was done by hand. You can try stirring up a batch yourself.

TRY THIS

Homemade ice cream
You'll need:
500 mL (2 c) cold 18% cream
125 mL (½ c) white sugar
2 mL (½ tsp) vanilla
plastic jug or similar container
1 dixie cup, 150 mL (4 oz)
1 styrofoam cup, 300-350 mL (8-10 oz)
clean snow or finely crushed ice
60 mL (4 Tbsp) table salt or coarse salt
2 stir sticks
thermometer that can measure below freezing
  (optional)

1. Mix the cream, sugar and vanilla together in the jug.
2. Pour some cream mixture into the dixie cup, filling it half to three-quarters full. Keep it cold.
3. Fill the styrofoam cup about one-third full with snow or ice. If you have a thermometer, measure the temperature of the ice.
4. Add about 45-60 mL (3 - 4 Tbsp) of salt to the ice. Stir. (Mark the stir stick you use so you won't mistakenly use it in the ice cream mix.) Measure the temperature of the ice again.
5. Make a hole in the icy slush big enough for the dixie cup and sit the cup in it so that ice comes up around the sides but doesn't get into the mixture.
6. Using the clean stir stick, stir the ice cream mixture slowly, scraping the newly formed crystals from the bottom and sides of the cup and stopping from time to time to let the ice cream solidify. You may have to stir on and off for 20-30 minutes until the ice cream is ready to eat—icy and only slightly soft. If you want to try other flavours, add a little chocolate syrup or other flavouring to the ice cream when it's at the slushy stage.

Why do you use salt water to freeze the ice cream?
Ice cream mix starts to freeze at -3° C (27° F), so your container has to be cooled below that. You could use solid ice from the freezer but the warm room air, the relative warmth of the ice cream mix and friction from the stirring would soon melt it around the inner container. Since ordinary water freezes at 0° C (32° F), even melted ice water is warmer than 0° C and too warm to freeze ice cream.

Salt water, though, has a lower freezing temperature than plain water. When you put salt and ice together you create a mix that can stay cold enough to freeze your ice cream.

Snow or crushed ice

Ice cream mixture

What's in that ice cream, anyway?

You might expect that the more you pay for a food, the more ingredients it would have. Ice cream is just the opposite.

Most premium-priced ice creams have the same ingredients you used in your experiment—cream, sugar, flavouring and air. Some of them may also add an egg, which not only makes a richer ice cream, but acts as an emulsifier, keeping the milk fat droplets separated and distributed evenly throughout the mix. This makes the ice cream smoother.

In cheaper ice cream, emulsifiers such as mono- and diglycerides substitute for eggs. And whey, a byproduct of cheesemaking, can substitute for some of the cream or milk. Artificial vanilla or other flavours can replace the real thing.

Then there are stabilizers, such as gelatin, carob, guar gum and carrageenan. These keep ice crystals from forming as ice cream warms and cools in the trip from manufacturer to your fridge and again every time you open the freezer door. All of these ingredients can change the flavour and texture of ice cream.

You can see what the stabilizers do to ice cream. All you need is some homemade ice cream (or a premium brand with just the basic ingredients) and some ice cream with as many stabilizers as possible. Spoon the same amount of each ice cream into separate dishes and let them melt. What are the differences? Which one would you rather slurp out of the bowl?

73

KEEPING IT

DID you ever wonder why you have a refrigerator? No, it's not just to hum along with you when you want to sing a duet. It's to make sure that when you want food, something else hasn't gotten to it first! If you keep food cold, microrganisms such as bacteria, moulds and yeasts don't grown as quickly. If they don't grow, your food doesn't spoil.

People were thinking up ways to keep food long before there were refrigerators. A lot of the old methods are still being used. Smoking meats, such as ham and bacon, is a method that's been around for years. Adding salt to foods and pickling are also ways of preserving foods. Today, new techniques are being developed all the time, such as retort pouches to cook food in a bag.

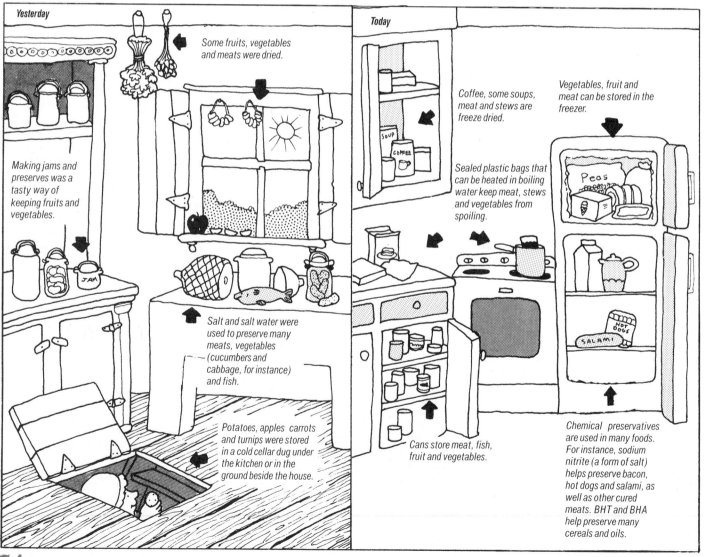

Yesterday

Some fruits, vegetables and meats were dried.

Making jams and preserves was a tasty way of keeping fruits and vegetables.

Salt and salt water were used to preserve many meats, vegetables (cucumbers and cabbage, for instance) and fish.

Potatoes, apples carrots and turnips were stored in a cold cellar dug under the kitchen or in the ground beside the house.

Today

Coffee, some soups, meat and stews are freeze dried.

Sealed plastic bags that can be heated in boiling water keep meat, stews and vegetables from spoiling.

Vegetables, fruit and meat can be stored in the freezer.

Cans store meat, fish, fruit and vegetables.

Chemical preservatives are used in many foods. For instance, sodium nitrite (a form of salt) helps preserve bacon, hot dogs and salami, as well as other cured meats. BHT and BHA help preserve many cereals and oils.

TRY THIS

Banana chips

Try preserving a banana by drying it. People used to dry fruits, vegetables and meat in the sun for days. You can speed up the process (and prevent insects getting into your bananas) by asking your parents if you can use the oven.

You'll need:
a firm, but fresh, ripe banana
knife
lemon juice
a cookie sheet

1. Peel the banana and cut it into slices about 0.5 cm (¼ inch) thick.
2. Dip the banana pieces into lemon juice to keep them from turning brown. Lemon juice also preserves flavour and vitamins.
3. Preheat the oven to 60° C (140° F). If you can't set it this low, place the lower rack at least 20 cm (8 inches) from the bottom of the oven. Don't make the oven too hot or the bananas will cook instead of drying.
4. Spread the banana slices in a single layer on a cookie sheet. Place the sheet in the oven and close the door. Turn the bananas over about every half hour, until they don't stick to the sheet anymore. Then, stir them about every half hour.
5. In about 7 hours, take two pieces out and let them cool. If they're done, they'll be pliable and the pieces shouldn't stick together. Make a cut in one piece. You shouldn't be able to squeeze any moisture out of it. If they're not quite done, dry them in the oven for up to another hour. Test them once in a while for doneness.

When the banana chips have cooled, store them in a plastic bag with as much air taken out as possible. You can do this by putting a straw in the bag opening, holding the bag tightly around the straw and sucking all the air out. Hold the bag tightly shut so the air doesn't get back in and fasten it with a twist tie.

HAVE you ever been on a camping trip where you had to bring all your food? After a few days, meals get boring and if you're a long way from a store, you're likely to run out of some things. Taking food on a trip has always been a big problem. Sometimes, it's even been a nightmare.

It was a nightmare in 1521 for the famous Spanish seafarer and explorer, Ferdinand Magellan, and his crew on the ship, *Victoria*.

When Magellan started his voyage to sail across the Pacific Ocean to find spices and other valuables, he prepared for it like all the other sea captains of that era.

He loaded the ship with fresh fruits—mainly lemons and oranges—to prevent scurvy. But they were gone within the first few weeks.

The ship also carried a lot of garlic because sailors believed it would keep them healthy. It also improved the taste of the salted meat, dried fish and unleavened bread and biscuits that made up the menu.

You ate the meat, fish and biscuits cold in the morning, hot at lunch and cold again at dinner—the same thing, day after day after day. You washed it down with watered-down wine.

After a few weeks at sea, the wine went bad and turned into vinegar. But you drank it anyway. It took your mind off how miserable you were feeling. It helped you ignore the rats, lice, worms and weevils that infested and ruined your food. It made it easier to swallow the rats you ate—when you could catch them. It also helped you forget the pain of scurvy, a disease in which your gums bled and joints swelled and you became very weak because there were no fresh fruits or vegetables in your diet.

When you started your adventure you knew that your food would go bad within a few weeks. It was a risk you took if you wanted to be an explorer and adventurer, if you wanted the wealth a successful voyage could bring you. All you could do was hope to reach land and get more food and fresh water before you died.

Antonio Pigafetta was with Magellan on that voyage and recorded it in his diary. Here is what it was like at its worst:

"We remained three months and 20 days without taking on board provisions or any other refreshments, and we ate only old biscuit turned to powder, all full of worms and stinking of the urine the rats had made on it, having eaten the good. And we drank water impure and yellow. We ate ox hides, which were very hard because of the sun, rain and wind."

The stories told by Pigafetta and other survivors of that trip weren't too different from those told by other adventurers and explorers. Even today's space adventurers don't get the food of their dreams.

Magellan's shopping list	
What Magellan took to feed 200 men on his voyage across the Pacific.	
flour	363 kg (800 lbs)
garlic buds	250 strings
cheese	1278 kg (2820 lbs)
honey	614 kg (1350 lbs)
almonds	35 L (1 bushel)
anchovies	150 barrels
sardines	10 000
raisins	850 kg (1870 lbs)
prunes	90 kg (198 lbs)
beans	106 L (3 bushels)

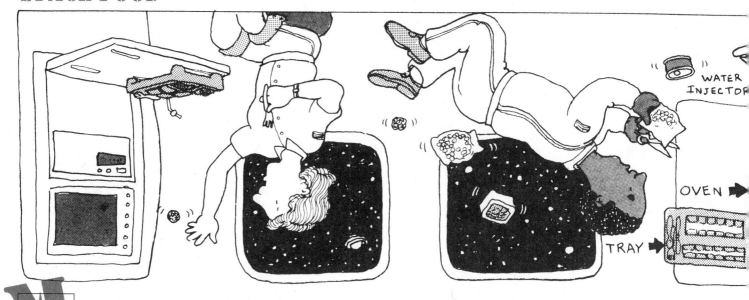

MAGELLAN's crew might have had to battle with scurvy on their long ocean voyages but you can bet they never had to chase a flying meatball for dinner. That problem is part of life for today's long-distance travellers, the astronauts. Because there's no gravity in space, things don't stay where you put them. And that makes cooking and eating tricky.

The first astronauts solved the problem of flyaway food by squeezing their meals out of tubes. The food looked like baby food—and tasted worse.

Fortunately, space food technology has improved since then. If you could float into a space shuttle kitchen at dinner time and join the crew for a meal, here's what you'd find.

Meal preparation starts 30 to 60 minutes before you want to eat. You would begin by washing your hands, just like you do at home. But instead of sloshing them in a sink, you'd scrub up in a "hand wash hygiene station" that looks like a goldfish bowl.

Don't head for the refrigerator next because there isn't one. Instead, food is put in sealed packages called retort pouches that don't need to be refrigerated. These packages are also specially designed to stand up to the vibration, temperature, acceleration and pressure in a space flight.

You'd have foods that look and taste just like Earth foods—hot dogs, applesauce, mixed vegetables and fruit cocktail. You might even get shortbread cookies for dessert, if you had been good and finished all your experiments. Space cookies, though, are much smaller than regular Earth cookies. They're exactly bite size, so they fit into your mouth all at once and don't leave crumbs floating around to get into the machinery. Other foods, such as rye bread and nuts, are exactly like the Earth version.

Many space foods, such as scrambled eggs, are freeze dried—that is, they have all the moisture removed from them. Why? They weigh less without all that water and they can be packed in handy individual pouches to make preparation easier. Before eating, you would rehydrate (add water to) the food in these pouches by sticking a hollow needle connected to a water supply into the pouch and squirting in a specified amount of water.

To cook your food, you wouldn't use a stove or an oven with electric or gas heat like those you have at home. You wouldn't even use a microwave oven. All food would be heated in a convection, or forced hot air, oven. It can heat up to $82°C$ ($180°F$) and hold your meal at $65°C$ ($150°F$) for a long time.

When it's time to serve supper, you and the other astronauts would cut open the food bags with scissors. Eating can be another problem, though. What happens when your plate decides it won't stay where you put it and wants to take a little side trip? You use

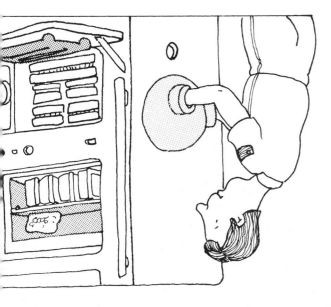

Velcro to fasten your tray to your knees or a table. You even have special foot and thigh restraints to tie yourself down for a meal. After all, it's rude to keep floating away from the table!

When you eat in space, food sticks to a spoon because of the moisture in it. But you have to eat slowly. Move too fast and it comes unstuck and drifts away. Meatballs on the ceiling again!

Clean up is a lot easier than at home. You would clean off the serving tray and utensils with disposable wipes, then store them for the next meal. The other dishes would be thrown out, which puts an end to the argument over whose turn it is to wash.

TRY THIS

Space food on Earth

You don't need to travel in space to try some space food. Look for some space food in your supermarket. You can buy prepared foods in the same kind of retort pouches that astronauts use in space. They need no refrigeration and are sold off the shelf like cans. Look for flat cardboard boxes containing foods such as chili, ravioli, chicken à la king, etc. They don't look like much, but they could be out of this world.

Space pop

You've probably let go of an inflated balloon and watched it go whizzing around the room propelled by escaping air. Imagine what it would be like to have a pop can zooming around propelled by escaping soda. Where could that happen? In space.

For years, the danger—and mess—that carbonated and pressurized beverages could cause in zero gravity prevented astronauts from having pop in space.

Then scientists at two of the major soft drink companies took time away from other serious research (such as creating cherry cola) to design the world's first space pop cans. One company spent $250,000 on the project.

The space cans have special valves and nozzles to make sure that the drink goes directly into your mouth under a comfortable pressure.

Of course, pop in space will not really be practical until they solve two other major problems: how to safely make popcorn in zero gravity and finding a pizza parlour that will deliver a double cheese, double pepperoni in orbit.

PROCESS YOUR OWN CHEESE

WHEN was the last time you had spoiled food for lunch? If you like cheese, probably not that long ago. Cheese was discovered centuries ago. According to legend, an Arab travelling across the desert decided to take some milk along with him. He poured it into a pouch he had made out of the stomach of a lamb.

He made the journey, but the milk didn't, at least not the way he had planned. When he arrived, he found not liquid milk, but chunky milk. He didn't know what had happened, but he was hungry, so he ate it. What a surprise! Spoiled milk tasted good!

The warm desert sun had changed the milk, with a little help from rennet, a substance found in the lamb's stomach where the milk was stored. Rennet helps young animals digest food. It combined with the milk and helped it to curdle. The rocking motion of the camel going up and down sand dunes churned the milk in the pouch. In three shakes of a lamb's stomach, they had cheese!

Famous Cheeses

If you're a mouse, cheese is cheese. But people tend to have favourites. Here's how three popular cheeses are made:

- People get wrinkles when they get older. Swiss cheese gets holes. During the aging process, special bacteria in the cheese give off a gas that makes big bubbles. Slice through a bubble and you get a piece of cheese with a hole. And you thought mice had been eating it!
- Cheddar cheese is cooked and drained like other cheeses and then it's "cheddared" or matted. That means the cheese is cut into slabs that are turned frequently and piled in layers to dry.
- If you put process cheese slices in a mousetrap, would you catch a process mouse? Actually, process cheese slices are made of real cheese mixed with milk powder and other ingredients, then heated and allowed to cool. The extra ingredients in process cheese help keep the oil from separating and also prevent the cheese from changing texture or going rubbery when it's heated. This process preserves the cheese and makes it cheaper to produce.

You can find out the difference between process and regular cheese with this experiment. Make two grilled cheese sandwiches, one with process cheese slices and the other with regular mild cheddar. Cut the finished sandwiches into pieces and mix them up, then try to pick out the process cheese pieces from the regular ones by their texture and appearance. Which one is chewier?

TRY THIS

Make your own cheese

You'll need:
125 mL (½ c) homogenized milk
small saucepan
two large clear glasses (plastic or glass)
an eye dropper
liquid rennet (available at health food stores)
stir stick
piece of cheesecloth 15 cm (6 inches) square

1. Warm the milk in the saucepan over low heat, stirring occasionally. Every couple of minutes, test the temperature of the milk by putting a drop of it on your inner wrist or arm. Test more frequently as the milk heats up. When the milk feels the same temperature as your skin, remove it from the heat.
2. Pour the milk into one of the glasses.
3. Using the dropper, add 4 or 5 drops of rennet to the milk.
4. Stir the milk briefly.
5. Stop stirring and wait about 20 minutes.
6. When you notice a clear, yellowish liquid, called whey, covering the surface of the mix, tip the glass. If the thickened milk, now called curds, breaks away from the sides of the glass, it's ready.
7. Place the cheesecloth over the mouth of the full glass. Hold the cheesecloth securely and turn the glass upside down over the empty glass. Let the liquid pour through into the empty glass. Now you have a cheesecloth full of curds and a glass full of whey. (Where's Miss Muffet when you need her?)
8. Hold the curds in the cheesecloth and squeeze the excess whey from them, letting it drip into the glass.
9. Open the cheesecloth. The small lump of white stuff is cheese. Taste it. If it's too bland, try adding a bit of salt. Most of the cheese you're used to eating has been aged to bring out the flavour.
10. Before you throw out your leftover whey, you might want to taste it. A great deal of whey is produced by the cheese-making industry. Most of it is used in animal feed, but some is also used as a milk substitute in many human foods. You often find it included in lower priced ice cream, for instance. How do you think it would affect the taste?

INSIDE STORY OF A CHOCOLATE BAR

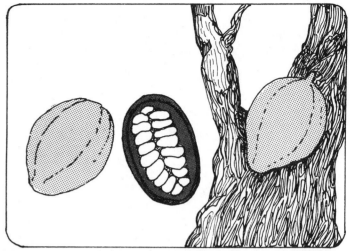

RIDDLE: What grows on trees, is shaped like a melon and is full of beans?

Answer: Cacao pods, used to make the world's favourite treat—chocolate.

You find the yellow, red or green pods on the branches or trunks of cacao trees in warm countries like Brazil and Africa's Ivory Coast. After picking, you split the pods open with a sharp machete or knife. Inside, you find not chocolate but about 30 white beans.

You pile the beans on the ground, cover them with banana leaves and let them ferment for several days until they become brownish-red. Then you spread them out in the sun and dry them.

Bags of the dried beans are sent to chocolate factories. After cleaning and roasting, the shells are quite brittle and loose and the beans smell like chocolate. Next the beans are put through a machine that removes the shells and cracks the beans into small pieces, called nibs. Another machine grinds the nibs into a fine paste, called chocolate liquor.

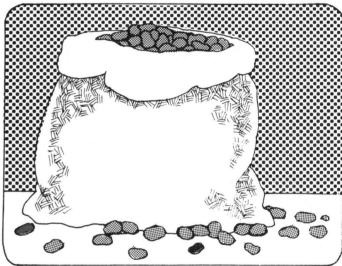

If you just let chocolate liquor harden, you'll have baking chocolate. But there are two other things you can do with chocolate liquor—turn it into eating chocolate or separate it into its two ingredients, cocoa and cocoa butter.

When you mix chocolate liquor with extra cocoa butter and sugar, you get dark eating chocolate. If you add milk to the chocolate liquor, along with the extra cocoa butter and sugar, you get milk chocolate. If you don't use any chocolate liquor at all, but just mix cocoa butter with milk and sugar, you get "white chocolate," which isn't really chocolate at all because it doesn't contain any chocolate liquor.

Although this may sound quite simple, the actual amount of each ingredient is a closely guarded secret at a chocolate factory. No company wants anyone to know how their own special brand of chocolate is made.

TRY THIS

A chocolate bar of your own

You'll need:

25 mL (2 Tbsp) powdered cocoa (the stuff you use to make cocoa from scratch)

25 mL (2 Tbsp) of sugar (table sugar is good, but fruit sugar produces a smoother result)

5 mL (1 tsp) of unsalted butter or vegetable shortening

a double boiler

wax paper

1. Put enough water in the bottom of the double boiler to just touch the top half when it's in place. Remove the top half and bring the water to a boil on the stove.

2. Turn off the heat and put the top half of the double boiler into place.

3. Put the cocoa, sugar and butter or shortening together into the top of the double boiler and stir until the mixture is smooth and the sugar is dissolved.

4. Spread the wax paper on a counter near the stove.

5. Carefully remove the top of the double boiler and pour the chocolate mixture onto the wax paper. Let it harden and taste.

If you made your chocolate with vegetable shortening, try another batch with butter. If you used butter, try vegetable shortening. Which do you prefer? You can experiment with the taste by slightly changing the proportions of cocoa, sugar and butter or shortening.

WHOLE HOG

DOES your room look as though a pig lives there? One probably does—or parts of a pig, anyway.

There's more to a pig than just bacon. Pig parts help clean your teeth, style your hair, keep your hands warm and even paint a room. As the pork producers like to brag: We use everything but the squeal.

TRY THIS

Where's the pig?

Have a scavenger hunt with some of your friends and see who can collect the most pig products in 10 minutes. Here are just a few things that started out with four hoofed feet and a curly tail.

1. Look in lists of ingredients for "fatty acids" and "glycerol." They're produced by cooking the inedible parts of a pig, such as trimmings and bones. You'll find them in:

hand or foundation cream	face cream	lipstick
	cream rouge	shaving cream
	bubble bath	soap
shampoo	mouthwash	paint
toothpaste	throat lozenges	jar of blowing type bubbles

2. You can tell that leather or suede is true pigskin by the groups of three tiny holes you find all over the surface. Look for the pig in:

glove	purse	binocular case
car seat	shoe	

3. You can probably even find some of the hair of a pig's chinny chin chin. Look at:

nail brush	toothbrush	shaving brush
hair brush	clothes brush	bath brush
paint brush		

4. Don't forget about food in your hunt for a sign of swine. Parts of pig pop up inside potables you never knew came from pigs. These have gelatin in them, a product made when pigskin is cooked in hot water. The gelatin is used for thickening in:

marshmallows	gelatin desserts (such as Jello)	canned meats
yogurt		sour cream
cottage cheese		ice cream

Other things with gelatin in them include:

crepe paper	film	wave set lotion
capsules for drugs	carbonless paper	

Pigs to the rescue

Pigs have even saved people's lives. People with defective heart valves have had pig heart valves implanted to replace their own.

Other pig organs are used to make drugs, such as insulin for diabetics and heparin for preventing blood clots. Pigskin is used as a temporary dressing for burns.

The glycerine from our porcine friends is even used to make dynamite! What an explosive personality for someone who likes taking mud baths to keep cool!

INSIDE STORY OF POPCORN

POPCORN has been around for a long time, even before the movies. The Incas used it for decoration hundreds of years ago, and the Native People of North America introduced the Pilgrims to it at the first Thanksgiving dinner ever held.

One of the nicest things about popcorn is that you can eat as much as you want of it and all it'll spoil is your appetite. A mug full of plain popcorn has just a bit of protein and fat, some fibre that you need in your diet and only 25 calories.

If you've popped popcorn, though, you've probably noticed that some batches come out fluffier and softer than others. Why? The secret's inside the kernel.

If you carefully cut a kernel of popping corn in half, you would see that it's very tightly packed with softer, slightly moist material. The kernel is really the seed of a new corn plant, and the moisture sealed inside helps keep it alive until conditions are right for sprouting. The moisture is what makes the corn pop.

If the kernel is heated very quickly, the moisture vaporizes into steam and expands rapidly, exerting enough pressure to burst the kernel open. When the tight jacket of the kernel bursts, the material inside expands, rather like a released jack-in-the-box springing to its full height.

How important is that internal drop of water for producing good popcorn? Here's an experiment you can munch through.

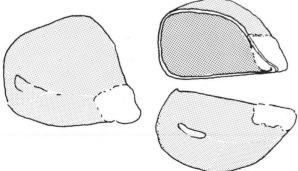

TRY THIS
The popcorn test

You'll need:
about 125 mL (½ c) fresh popping corn
a cookie sheet
a ruler

1. Measure out 50 mL (¼ c) of kernels of corn and count them. Count out another batch with the same number of kernels.
2. Preheat the oven to 100° C (200° F). Spread one batch of corn kernels out on the cookie sheet and put them in the oven for 90 minutes.
3. While they're heating, pop the other batch of kernels. Count the number of kernels that **don't** pop, then measure the length of ten of the popped ones. Choose the ten at random—just stick your hand into the bowl and take a bunch. Add up the measurements and divide by ten to find their average size. Write down your findings so you don't forget them.
5. Keep your notes and eat the popcorn.
6. After 90 minutes, remove the heated kernels from the oven and let them cool. Then pop them the same way as the first batch. Again, count the unpopped kernels and measure ten of the ones that pop. Eat a kernel or two and compare with the first batch.
7. Eat the rest and try to figure out what caused the difference between the two batches of popcorn. (Clue: water evaporates in heat.)

What do you think would happen if you soaked stale popping corn in water before popping it?

KITCHEN MAGIC

 OU can be a magician. All you need is some food! A lot of the everyday things in your kitchen can produce magical effects.

TRY THIS

Magic potion
Try mixing up this amazing potion for your friends.

You'll need
15 mL (1 Tbsp) baking soda
water
15 mL (1 Tbsp) vinegar
large glass

1. Mix the baking soda with the water in the glass.
2. Add the vinegar. (A few magic words will make things more dramatic.)
3. Stand back and watch.

How does it work?
One of the most common "magical" reactions in the kitchen happens when you mix an acid (such as vinegar, lemon juice or buttermilk) and a base (such as baking soda). Acids and bases shake things up wherever they go. One of the nice things they do is make gas when you mix them. The bubbles they produce make things like pancakes rise and become light and fluffy. Without them, you'd have concrete cakes!

Too much of one or the other can cause chemical reactions in certain foods—with fun results.

Rainbow brew
Here's some more magic brewing with acids and bases.

You'll need:
grape juice (*not* grape drink!)
15 mL (1 Tbsp) baking soda dissolved in 125 mL (½ c) water
15 mL (1 Tbsp) vinegar dissolved in 125 mL (½ c) water
large glass

1. Half fill the glass with grape juice.
2. Slowly pour in some of the baking soda mixture.
3. Watch what happens.
4. Slowly pour in some of the vinegar solution.
5. Try alternating them.

How does it work?
Ordinary (white) light is made up of many different colours. Depending on their molecular structure, objects absorb some, all or none of the colours of white light that hit them. The colours that aren't absorbed are reflected or passed through the object and eventually reach your eyes. The colour you see depends on which colours bounced off or passed through the object. Grape juice absorbs all the colours of white light except those that make you see purple. When you add one of your "magic" mixtures to the grape juice, you change its molecular structure, which also changes the colours that it absorbs and reflects.

Magic egg predictor
If you don't do the next magic trick right, you'll really lay an egg.

You'll need:
1 hard-boiled egg
1 uncooked egg

1. Hand a friend the two eggs and announce that you can tell the cooked egg from the raw one without even cracking the shell.
2. Put one egg at a time on a table and spin it. If it goes fast, crack it open on top of your head—it's the hard cooked one! If it spins slowly and stops quickly DON'T CRACK IT ON YOUR HEAD or the yolk will be on you.

How does it work?
The secret is in the spin. A hard-boiled egg is solid and spins as a unit. In a raw egg, you spin the shell, but the shell has to start moving the liquidy insides. This uses up energy so the egg spins slowly.

Baked ice cream
Would it take magic to bake ice cream without melting it? No. You can do it and surprise everyone with the results.

You'll need:
3 egg whites
125 mL (½ c) sugar
a big, thick, hard cookie (Chinese almond cookies work well)
250 mL (1 c) ice cream
baking sheet
aluminum foil

1. Heat oven to 260° C (500° F).
2. Cover the baking sheet with aluminum foil.
3. Beat egg whites (do not put in the egg yolks) until they form soft peaks.
4. Add sugar to the beaten egg whites, 15 mL (1 Tbsp) at a time, beating the egg whites after each addition.

5. Continue to beat the egg whites and sugar until the mixture is thick and glossy looking. This is called meringue.
6. Put the cookie on the baking sheet. Place some frozen ice cream on top of the cookie, so that it fits without hanging over the edge of the cookie.
7. Spread meringue thickly all over the ice cream like icing on a cake, covering it completely. Make sure there are no exposed spots!
8. Bake on the lowest rack of the oven for 3 to 5 minutes until the meringue is light brown. Watch it closely so it doesn't burn.
9. Take it out of the oven and dig in!

How does it work?
The meringue acts something like an insulated foam drinking cup, the insulation in a house or a down-filled coat. They all have small air spaces trapped in them that slow down the passage of heat or cold.

The meringue works the same way. Beating the egg whites made lots of air bubbles in the meringue. When you spread the meringue over the ice cream, you insulate it so the heat can't get in during the short time it's in the oven.

If meringue were permanent and didn't melt (or get eaten) you could probably use it to insulate a drinking cup, a house, even you. Imagine wearing a meringue parka to school. If you forgot your lunch, you could just eat your coat!

89

INSIDE STORY OF POP

WHAT's the formula for soda pop? It could be F + F = P (Fizz plus Flavour equals Pop).

Pop began as fizzy water that people added flavouring to. Why did they want fizzy water to start with? Because they thought it was healthy, just as they believed the bubbly waters of natural springs had powers to cure them of all sorts of ills.

Although the first artificial bubbly water was made in 1722, it wasn't until 1832 that carbonated beverages became really popular. That's when John Matthews invented a machine to inject carbonated gas into water.

People then started experimenting with adding flavour to the bubbly water to give it more taste. They also added the bubbly water to some of the beverages and potions they already had, to make them taste better. Within a short time, the familiar pops of today were developed—from colas to ginger ales. Of course, not all tastes were popular. For some reason, spinach and eggplant soda pop never caught on.

TRY THIS

Make your own ginger ale

You'll need:

180 mL (¾ c) peeled, grated ginger root
a large glass jar with lid
1 L (4 c) cold water
another large jar or bowl
a wire strainer
a coffee filter (nylon or paper)
sugar

1. Place the grated ginger in the glass jar. Add the cold water and put the lid on the jar. Let it sit for 24 hours.
2. Pour the liquid through the wire strainer into a bowl. Rinse out the jar you steeped the ginger in and throw away the ginger.
3. Pour the liquid through the coffee filter back into the clean jar.
4. Add sugar a little at a time until it's sweet enough for you. Try it plain or mixed with soda water. Do a "taste test" with your family and friends. Which way do most people prefer it?

ANSWERS

The Case of the Missing Teeth: 1 fox, 2 deer, 3 anteater, 4 seal, 5 human.

A Detective Story: 1 The pudding has about 800 mg of salt, the peanuts have about 600 mg of salt and the o-shaped oat cereal has about 300 mg of salt.
2 The ketchup has about 80 mL (17 teaspoons) of sugar, the flavoured yogurt has about 40 mL (7½ teaspoons) of sugar and the cola has about 30 mL (6½ teaspoons) of sugar.

That Sinking Feeling: 1 baked beans 11 g, 2 shredded wheat biscuits 6.1 g, 3 raw carrot 3.7 g, 4 apple 3.1 g, 5 whole wheat bread 2.4 g, 6 white bread 0.8 g, 7 grapes 0.4 g, 8 egg, none.

Choose a Meal:
Meal A has 999 calories in it. About one-tenth are from protein, and the rest are divided equally between fats and carbohydrates. Not a well-balanced meal—it's too low in protein and too high in fat.
Meal B has 867 calories in it. It gets about a quarter of its calories from proteins, nearly half from carbohydrates and almost a third from fat. A pretty good choice, even though it's a bit too high in protein.
Meal C has 958 calories in it. It's just right in protein but gets less than half its calories from carbohydrates and almost half from fats. Not a well-balanced meal.
The best choice? Meal B.

Guess the Food: 1 ketchup, 2 marshmallows, 3 chewing gum, 4 jelly beans, 5 orange.

INDEX